FIRE AND ICE

Lord Richard Swynford pulled Katherine to him. She could feel the strength in the hard muscles in his chest and in the arms encircling her waist as his mouth covered hers.

Then he tore himself away. "God, what am I about?" he mumbled in disbelief.

"I know we can't," Katherine said. "It is wrong, horribly wrong. I should not be here."

"Then why the devil are you?" he said, his voice raging with frustration. He swept her an elegant, savagely mocking bow. "Goodnight, adventuress."

"Adventuress! How dare you," Katherine shouted back, and her hand delivered a stinging slap to the cheek that a moment ago she had longed to stroke.

As far as Katherine was concerned, that should have been the end of it. But, as any student of life and love would wager, it was only the beginning. . . .

ROMANTIC INTERLUDES

My Lady Adventuress

by

Roberta Eckert

A SIGNET BOOK

NEW AMERICAN LIBRARY

Copyright ©1987 by Roberta Eckert

SIGNET TRADEMARK REG. U.S.PAT. OFF. AND FOREIGN COUNTRIES
REGISTERED TRADEMARK—MARC REGISTRADA
HECHO EN CHICAGO, U.S.A.

SIGNET, SIGNET CLASSIC, MENTOR, ONYX, PLUME, MERIDIA
and NAL BOOKS are published by NAL PENGUIN INC.,
1633 Broadway, New York, New York 10019

First Printing, June, 1987

1 2 3 4 5 6 7 8 9

To Nana
who believed and encouraged

Chapter 1

Katherine Spencer met Giles Swynford in church. Actually, noticed Giles would be more to the point. Giles, like every other male in Dover between sixteen and sixty, had noticed Miss Spencer long before.

On the particular Sunday, Katherine was proudly wearing a charming new poke bonnet that perfectly matched her enormous blue eyes. She knew the bonnet, which had been brought into fashion by the Grand Duchess of Oldenburg, was most flattering.

Katherine had heard how the formidable duchess had actually invaded an all-male banquet in Guildhall given by the Regent, in honor of her brother, Czar Alexander. The grand duchess had insisted the music be halted because it gave her a headache. It was only with much persuasion that she allowed "God Save the King" to be played for the toast. Imagining the scene that the duchess must have created, Katherine smiled to herself, delighted by the audacity of a woman who could actually carry out such outrageous demands. At that moment she happened to raise her eyes to those of Captain Swynford's. Giles, thinking that her dazzling, merry smile was meant for him, felt flattered and responded with a gleam of interest and a courtly nod.

Katherine was taken by surprise, and quickly turned her head to listen to Vicar Denniston, a blush stealing up her cheeks. She realized the dashing captain assumed her smile was directed at him. Her telltale blush afforded Captain Swynford a great deal of satisfaction.

Under veiled lashes, she stole another glance at the tall young man in House Guard uniform. With his athletic build, tawny hair, and gold-brown eyes, he was one of the most handsome men she had ever seen. Quickly Katherine returned her eyes to her prayer book, not wanting her father to notice her inquisitive gaze.

Standing at her side, Dr. Spencer had indeed observed the exchange. Though it amused him, it also brought forcibly to mind a nagging concern that had begun to cause him a measure of anxiety for some time. He must do something about Katherine's future, he thought. He had been careless, and the days had slipped by all too swiftly. What he had intended and failed to take action on "tomorrow" had come to haunt him today. Katherine was twenty and should have been given a season. Long ago. He shook his head in self-reproach and turned his attention to Vicar Denniston's sermon.

Giles hastily looked toward the pulpit also, assuming that the frown he had seen upon the face of the young lady's father had been directed at him.

After the service ended, he maneuvered his way through the crowded church toward Katherine and her father. Overtaking them at the entrance, he favored them with his most charming smile. "Good day," he greeted them.

"Good day to you, Captain. House Guards, is it?" replied Dr. Spencer in rather good humor.

"Aye, Coldstream, but it seems as though I've missed the war with Boney safe in Elba," he answered in obvious disappointment.

"War is nothing to regret missing, lad. If you had seen the casualties I've cared for here in Dover, you'd not be regretting it, to be sure."

Giles's attention, strayed to the beautiful young lady who stood beside her father. He wanted desperately to think of something clever to say. "I am Giles Swynford, sir. Northumberland is my home." This remark was hardly clever but allowed him time to fall into step with the couple.

"'Tis a long way from home, Captain. How do you like the southern coast?" Dr. Spencer asked as he approached their carriage.

"I like it fine, but nothing could compare to the haunting beauty of the north country or the magnificence of my family's country seat, Marston Hall," Captain Swynford said with sincere longing. "My brother is the Marquess of Marston," he added hastily, hoping to raise his status in their eyes, for he could see Dr. Spencer was about to assist his daughter into the carriage.

"Indeed," answered Dr. Spencer with a degree of interest usually reserved for concerned mamas with marriage for their daughters in mind. A thoughtful look came into his eyes.

"Captain Swynford, I am sure it's been a long time since you had some good home cooking. Perhaps you would like to join us one evening for dinner?"

Katherine's mouth fell open in surprise. Whatever possessed her father to invite this young man to dinner? A little feeling of delight and anticipation grew inside her as she cast another appreciative glance at the handsome Captain Swynford.

"I should be honored, doctor, and accept with great pleasure." Captain Swynford addressed Dr. Spencer, but his eyes never left Katherine's face.

Dr. Spencer chuckled with amusement as he asked the obviously smitten captain, "Would Tuesday evening be convenient?"

Captain Swynford nodded and vigorously shook Dr. Spencer's hand. "Indeed, Tuesday would be most convenient," he replied.

"Then we shall expect you at seven. Our home is

located at 3 Langdon Terrace," Paul Spencer explained as he began to assist Katherine into their carriage.

"Good day, Miss Spencer. Until Tuesday." Captain Swynford bowed, his light brown eyes dancing in delight.

On the homeward journey, Dr. Spencer and Katherine chatted about the weather, the sermon, and the countryside, which was now bleak with winter chill. No mention was made of young Captain Swynford. Katherine thought that fact, alone, spoke louder than any words.

After luncheon Dr. Spencer, as was his custom, retired to his study and his medical journals. Dr. Spencer had been trained at Oxford in the Royal College of Physicians, and like his peers, he discredited the knowledge possessed by surgeons, who were known only for their bloodletting, but lately had become interested in the Royal College of Surgeons, which had come into existence in 1800. It had been propelled into credibility by the eminent work of John Hunter and his remarkable anatomical collection. Dr. Spencer was a dedicated man who sought to improve his skill, for too often he had seen bungling by others who relied on the knowledge they already possessed and showed no desire to impove their abilities.

However, on this particular afternoon, Paul Spencer did not turn directly to his studies, but sat quietly in contemplation. A tall, spare man with a great shock of white hair, he gave the appearance of being more ascetic than he truly was. Great humor often twinkled from his blue eyes; he always felt an enormous kindness toward his fellow man, as well as a burning desire to ease pain whenever he could.

He was astute and knew he had placed his work above the needs of his daughter. He hadn't meant to, he had just become too concerned with his work. If only his wife Margaret had lived she would have seen that Katherine's future was secured. He shook his head, for not one day had passed since her death that he had not missed her. He had loved her so, and had thrown himself into his work as an effort to bury that ever-present pain.

But he did have Katherine, and she was a constant source of joy to him. They were comfortable together. She ran his home with competence and love; her natural gaiety and humor added so much to his lonely life.

He knew that in his desire to keep her with him he had unwisely protected her from the acquaintance of young men her own age. He realized that was wrong.

He had, on occasion, considered sending Katherine to her mother's relatives for a formal presentation. Margaret Spencer's sister, Cora, had married rather well and was connected to the Hollands. She could easily offer a season for Kate and had in fact done so, claiming Katherine's stunning looks could overcome her lack of wealth. Since there were many fine eligible gentlemen who did not need to choose a wife on the basis of her dowry but could easily afford a wife they desired for her charm alone, Katherine might do very well for herself. Cora had made it plain that Katherine was not getting any younger, and twenty, she had implied, was perilously close to being considered "too late."

Until now, he had rejected that scheme on Kate's own entreaty that she did not wish to go. But now he sat examining his reluctance, and he knew that it was because he would have simply missed her too much. That was a selfish motive, he admitted. Well, he thought, I shall make changes immediately. His impulsive invitation to the young Captain Swynford had been just the first step.

He would send her to her aunt in the spring. In the

meantime he had means of checking on the worthiness of the young captain. At least, for now, she would have another young person's company to enjoy.

Upstairs in her room, Kate twirled about in girlish delight. She paused before the mirror and critically examined her features, running her slender fingers along her face, turning her head this way and that, mentally appraising herself. She knew she was pretty but far underestimated her beauty. She criticized her full rosy mouth, unaware it was the kind of a mouth that a many a gentleman had contemplated kissing. Since Katherine had never had a serious suitor, she had received no flowery compliments or odes to her beauty. Her assessment was based only on what she perceived and, therefore, was without conceit.

Crossing her small, blue and white room, she threw herself on her chintz-covered bed and thought about the very handsome Captain Swynford. He could be considered no other way, with his tawny hair, smiling light brown eyes, and not least of all, his manly physique complimented so well by his dashing scarlet uniform.

Her heart beat faster as she contemplated his calling for dinner. Would she know what to say? He seemed so worldly and she was merely a doctor's daughter.

A frown flitted across her comely face as she dismally considered why he could possibly be interested in her. Had he merely accepted out of politeness? Remembering the encounter, she knew full well he had deliberately sought them out. Contented, she let anticipation fill her with delicious delight.

As he made his way to the King's Arms to meet his cardplaying comrades, Giles Swynford was more than a little pleased with his invitation to dine with the Spencers. Katherine Spencer certainly was a very taking young lady. Beautiful, he thought, a welcome diversion in this stinking town while he waited for his orders to come. A dissatisfied expression appeared on his classic features.

He luck certainly had been running poorly lately, but now, he thought, perhaps it was changing.

Chapter 2

The two days until Captain Swynford would call seemed an eternity to Katherine. She fussed over the menu, changing her mind at least a dozen times. The exasperated cook, Mrs. Powell, finally took matters into her own hands. Kindly shooing Katherine from the kitchen, she exclaimed loudly that she would take care of all the preparations.

Dr. Spencer observed the hustle and bustle with a small sense of self-satisfaction. It did his heart good to see Katherine so obviously happy and excited. His conscience was eased temporarily by the knowledge that he, at last, had taken a step to acquaint Katherine with someone her own age. Furthermore, his inquiries had revealed that Captain Swynford was from an illustrious family in the north. Dr. Spencer had also learned that the young man was well thought of by his commanding officer and comrades-in-arms. This information satisfied Dr. Spencer that he had acted correctly even if his invitation had been impulsive.

At last, Tuesday arrived. Katherine dressed with care. Her dark brown hair was washed and brushed until it shone with sleek gloss, then arranged so that soft ringlets framed her oval face. Her sky-blue eyes sparkled with anticipation and a faint pink glowed on her cheeks. Her water-silk gown of dusty rose displayed her feminine figure to advantage and her mother's pearls added the finishing touch to her dress. She took a final appraisal of herself in the mirror and twirled again in girlish delight, declaring herself well satisfied. Full of confidence and excitement, Katherine went downstairs to greet Giles.

He rose when she entered the room. She watched his smile light his face as he crossed the room to meet her halfway.

"Good evening, Miss Spencer. You are a pleasure to behold to this poor soldier's eyes. I hope I find you in good health," he said as he bent to kiss her extended hand.

"Thank you, Captain Swynford, and welcome to our home," she shyly replied.

Dr. Spencer smiled benignly upon the handsome pair. Taking up a crystal decanter, he offered them a glass of sherry, which they both accepted gratefully, for it served to ease the first awkward moments of such a meeting.

Captain Swynford raised his glass in a small salute and took a sip of the golden liquid. "Your sherry is excellent, Dr. Spencer. Contraband, I'd venture." He smiled with a knowing twinkle in his eyes.

"Many of my patients pay me with whatever they can. In this case, it proves an advantage to me, if not to the coffers of the crown," the doctor replied with a shrug. He raised his own glass in a responding salute and took a sip.

Giles chuckled and did likewise. "Well, soon enough the shipments from the Continent will be flowing freely." He sighed, not for the welcomed commodities that would be available but for the war that apparently had ceased.

"You regret so much then your lack of participation in the war?" Dr. Spencer asked with interest. The idea of wanting to serve in the military was foreign to his own nature.

Captain Swynford raised his eyes sharply. "Indeed I do, sir, for it would have . . ." His voice faded and his eyes took on a distant look. He straightened his relaxed posture and leaned slightly forward. "Never mind that," he said, waving his hand in a small gesture of dismissal. "We are all victims of our own circumstances. Do you not agree?" he asked cryptically.

Silence reigned for a moment. "Only to a point, Captain Swynford. We carry much of our own fate in our own hands," Dr. Spencer replied, not quite understanding the young Captain's remark. However, having lived long, and seen much suffering, he knew many problems charged to fate were the direct result of human action.

This unusual conversation was interrupted when Mrs. Black, the housekeeper, announced dinner was ready to be served.

Captain Swynford offered his arm to Katherine, who accepted it with a dazzling smile. Giles was momentarily taken aback by her uncommon beauty. A faraway, thoughtful look flickered across his face.

"It is indeed a pleasure to have this gracious invitation. One becomes lonely so far from home, and the warmth of your household is a most welcome change from my army quarters," he said with great sincerity as he escorted her into the dining room.

They dined on a light Dover sole in dill sauce, goose dressed with bread, raisins, and apples, and for dessert had crystallized custard with brandy sauce. Captain Swynford entertained them with amusing anecdotes about his efforts to keep his idle regiment happy, carefully avoiding the less savory aspects.

"Since we're not likely to fight the French anymore, it seems they'll have a go at one another. It's many a fight we've had to halt, so we drill frequently. That doesn't make them happy, but it reduces boredom and fisticuffs," he told them.

The conversation continued to be light and amusing as Captain Swynford displayed considerable charm and made much effort to include Katherine.

Their usual dinner guests were often men of science, and while Katherine had gained a vast medical knowledge simply by listening, this evening proved to be an exciting experience for her, for it was far more amusing.

"How long have you been in the army, Captain Swynford?" Dr. Spencer asked, still more than a little intrigued by the choice of a military career.

"Three years, sir. I do not mind the life. It allows me great freedom from my brother," he replied, and hastily added, "I hope to see the Continent yet. The war has gone on far too long and has drained too much from the English economy."

"And caused terrible carnage," Dr. Spencer heartily added.

Giles told them of his beloved Northumberland with fondness shining from his eyes. "But it is Marston Hall that I love most. However, all that has changed since Richard inherited," he said, a hint of complaint hanging on his words. Then, as if he had revealed too much, he changed the subject to the wonders of his family home.

"Marston Hall was actually a fortress at one time against the Scots. My ancestors lived in the hall but were prepared to defend against raids and indulge in a little raiding themselves. It is said that one ancestor commented that if he had not killed five Scots before breakfast, the day was wasted." He chuckled at the idea.

"When my mother and father were alive the hall was a lively and gracious place. Mother loved parties and the manor was often filled with guests and laughter. I remember hiding in the minstrels' gallery to watch the dancing. It was so happy then. It is just how I would have it today if it were in my power to do so." His voice trailed off and that distant expression appeared on his handsome face once more.

With obvious effort to change his thoughts he turned to Katherine, a boyish dimple appearing in his cheek. "The hills there are beautiful. They cast a purple haze along the horizon and in the spring and summer the hills are covered with heather and wild flowers," he said.

"Why, Captain, I do believe you are more poet than soldier," Katherine teased, her eyes laughing over the raised wineglass she placed against her lips.

"Perhaps, but I'm afraid my subject is somewhat singular," Giles admitted. "I do own a charming manor house called Merrywood Farms," he added as if by second thought.

"You seem to enjoy the country and the life it affords. I am surprised you have chosen the military life," Katherine commented.

An almost imperceptible frown crossed his brow and he paused as if to weigh his words. "I am the second son, as you know, and my brother is far too much the master. He does not accept my interference, so he purchased my colors for me."

Katherine sat and watched him a moment. "It is not your wish then?" she asked. "Wouldn't you wish to manage Merrywood? What a beautiful name—it sounds lovely."

Paul Spencer sent his outspoken daughter a warning look. He had carefully noted the handsome young captain's quick change of moods and sensed an underlying sadness in the charming young man. It seemed obvious to him that Captain Swynford was making the best out of an unhappy situation.

"The military life serves to place distance between my brother and me, and besides, I would like to see some of the world. I leave the management of Merrywood to my bailiff," he said cheerfully. "Actually, I had hoped to make the Continent before the war ended, but it is not to be so." He shrugged in fatalistic acceptance.

"I for one, am glad that you have missed the terrible war, as I am sure the rest of your family is," Katherine said gently, then lowered her eyes, feeling her color rising. Perhaps that had been too bold a remark, she thought.

"Indeed, Captain, we have seen too much of the damage done to the young men of our country. The glory of war is for the generals, not the men who must die or be maimed. I hold war to be the greatest scourge to mankind," Dr. Spencer said with vehemence. "Katherine will agree, for she has been called upon on many occasions to assist me in my work. It is no pretty sight."

Giles turned sharply to Katherine. "You mean, you have assisted your father in surgery? Unheard of!"

"How so, Captain? I am very capable," she replied.

"It is no fit service for a lady."

"Perhaps you are correct," Dr. Spencer said, "but my daughter's assistance often made a difference between life and death. I chose to take the course of saving any life I could. Katherine has grown up with medicine and is incalculably valuable in such situations. No doctor has been better served by a more competent assistant, I assure you."

"I beg your pardon, sir. I spoke from lack of knowledge . . . it just seems a lady of such—accept my pardon please."

"Done. You are not the first to express such an opinion," Paul Spencer replied. It was true he had been censured for allowing his daughter to assist him but until now it had never bothered him. Now he realized that the *ton* would place great censure on a lady serving in such a manner. He frowned.

Captain Swynford sought to change the subject. "Do you ride, Miss Spencer?"

"Gracious yes, it is one of my favorite pastimes. We

have wonderful views of the coast and the fresh smell of the sea makes it most pleasurable," Katherine responded.

"Dr. Spencer, may I have permission to ride with your daughter? If it is agreeable with Miss Spencer, of course," Giles said, turning his dimpled smile on the lady in question.

"Yes, I should like that. You will be impressed with the beauty of our vicinity. The north country does not hold all the beathtaking scenery, as you will see," she teased.

"You have my permission to ride, with Norton in attendance, of course. While you may not approve of my liberal attitude toward women, you can be assured I am most proper in the care of my daughter," Dr. Spencer said with some rancor.

Captain Swynford shifted in his chair, feeling slightly uncomfortable. "Of course. I would have expected no less." He turned again to Katherine. "If it is agreeable then, will you ride with me in the morning? I do not have duty until afternoon."

"Yes, Captain, I should like to do so," she said. The change in subject allowed the uncomfortable moment to pass.

The three sat after dinner in the family salon enjoying congenial conversation of a trivial nature. Declining any tea, Captain Swynford found it was soon time to take his leave. Katherine and her father escorted him to the front door.

"Thank you, once more, for the most pleasant evening I have had since I have joined the House Guards," he said, then bowed over Katherine's hand. His eyes met hers briefly, and she read the decided approval in them before he turned and left the house.

Wearing a deep blue riding habit and matching cape and hood lined with sable to protect her against the early March breeze, Katherine hurried down to the stables.

There she found Norton saddling the horses. A strong hulking man, long in service to Dr. Spencer, he was totally devoted to Katherine, for he had dandled her on his knee when she was but a wee child. He loved her as the daughter he never had. As a child, she had followed him everywhere, asking a myriad of questions which he had answered with great patience.

He was in his fifties, and had a ruddy complexion that indicated his Scotch heritage. His reddish hair was sprinkled with gray and crinkle lines ran from his clear blue eyes, denoting the amusement with which he viewed the world. His Calvinist upbringing had given him an acceptance of life but had not taken his joy of it. Norton was a man of great physical and character strength.

He was not an educated man, but he gave Katherine insight into the practical aspects of life, tinged with fateful acceptance. Valuable lessons for anyone, for often the advice of a man of common sense is far superior to that of sage philosophers. Katherine was therefore uniquely educated.

"Good morning, Norton. A beautiful day for a ride, even if spring has not yet brought us warmth."

"Indeed, Miss Kate, it is at that. However, I'm thinking 'tis the fine captain that makes the ride the more appealing," he teased.

"Do you now? My, my, you place too much importance on that fact!" she replied with a chuckle.

"Perhaps, perhaps . . . but it is more than the brisk air that places those roses in your cheeks, or I've missed my mark."

"You're too bold by far, Norton."

"Yes missy, I am that, but then who would I tease, if not you?"

Katherine laughed delightedly just as a horse entered

the stableyard. She turned to see Captain Swynford looking extremely handsome in scarlet coat and dark cape. He sat a magnificent stallion with a masculine assurance that was impressive.

Norton assisted Katherine into her saddle, giving her a knowing wink. Quickly, he mounted his own horse, moving with more swiftness than his extremely large frame might indicate possible.

Captain Swynford, noting Norton's powerful physique, understood Dr. Spencer's faith that Katherine was well protected. He smiled as he observed the large man, for though Katherine's outstanding beauty would always attract attention, she would be well served by so formidable a guard.

Giles smartly maneuvered his black stallion next to Katherine's chestnut and presented her with a small nosegay of violets attached to a slender gold filigree pin.

"A bit of spring to pin on your cape," he explained with boyish delight. With his tawny hair ruffled by the breeze, his light golden brown eyes gazing at her with admiration, and that elusive dimple brought out by his smile, he could not have been more appealing.

Completely captivated, she felt her heart skip a beat and let herself hold his gaze a moment. "Thank you, Captain, how thoughtful." She lowered her lashes as she pinned the delicate flowers on her cape, her fingers trembling ever so slightly. How exciting it was to have such attention, she thought. Like any young lady with a dashing gentleman at her side, she beamed with pleasure.

Giles watched her dark long lashes brush against her flushed cheeks. With satisfaction, he noted the sparkle of excitement in her blue eyes.

Katherine and Giles picked up their reins and rode out of the stableyard in high spirits, with Norton keeping enough distance behind to allow them to talk and flirt with ease. The morning was chilly with a misty breeze from the water, but the warmth between the two young people dispelled any cold. They laughed and raced along the track that overlooked the sea. Pointing out various points of interest, Katherine turned only to find Captain Swynford's eyes upon her. She blossomed under his flattering attention.

They rode along the track above the cliffs overlooking the sea. Gray and white waves crashed upon the rocks below. The gray sky reflected the sea, and gulls flew overhead calling in excited clamor. When Katherine raised her face to watch the soaring birds, her hood fell back, causing her dark curls to flutter against her cheek.

"You are very beautiful, Miss Spencer," Giles said, watching her. "How is it you have not long been spoken for?"

"You're too kind, sir. My life has been busy and I have not had much opportunity to meet suitable young men. Father wishes to send me to London this spring so that I might meet an eligible suitor. Aunt Cora has been after him to do so, but until now I had never wished to seek a husband," she replied with a frankness that was unusual in the young ladies of his acquaintance.

He laughed. "You are the most refreshing female I have ever met. Do you know, had I asked such a question to most young ladies, they would have simpered into a decline."

"Really? Why?"

"Good heavens, I do not know. I have very little patience with the missish maid." Again he laughed. "Tell me," he teased, "what did you mean by 'until now'?"

Katherine turned sharply away with a flush that gave away her embarrassment at the candor of her words. "I am afraid, Captain, I am not accustomed to the guarded small talk that must exist in the social circles you are used to. I see I shall have to learn quickly lest I find myself put continually to the blush.''

"Katherine, you're all that is charming and I truly enjoy your company." His voice suddenly changed. "I fear it grows late and I must return to duty." He purposefully turned his horse homeward.

The return trip was more subdued and conversation between them waned as Captain Swynford once again seemed preoccupied. It occurred to Katherine that he might have a fiancée at home. She dared not ask the question, but vowed to guard her thoughts more carefully.

Upon returning home, they bid farewell and Norton took the horses into the stable.

"I am in your debt once more. Thank you for a most enjoyable morning. May I call again?" the captain said, raising her hand to his mouth.

Katherine felt a thrill run through her as his lips gently brushed her cool skin. "Yes, Captain Swynford, you are welcome in our home. I also enjoyed this morning's ride," she said with slight formality.

The next morning a beautiful bouquet of yellow roses arrived from the captain. They were the first flowers Katherine ever received from a suitor and she glowed with excited happiness.

"Aren't they beautiful?" She giggled as Mrs. Black helped her arrange them in a blue glass vase and place them prominently on the hall console. All day long, Katherine stopped to smell them each time she passed through the hall.

Though he was pleased by Katherine's excitement, Dr. Spencer hoped she was not losing her heart too hastily to the dashing captain.

Chapter 3

The young captain continued to pay court to Katherine, calling at the Spencer home frequently. His visits were of short duration, as his duties demanded most of his time. Being young and healthy, he also enjoyed the more risqué pursuits that the sea port offered him and his military comrades. However, his thoughts frequently included Katherine.

His fellow officers, who had often seen the lovely Miss Spencer out walking with Giles, praised his outstanding luck in finding such a beautiful young lady.

Seated one evening with some fellow officers in the noisy, smoky King's Arms, Giles listened to the united opinions on the beauty of Miss Spencer. The conversation centered on the fact that he didn't deserve the luck in finding such an attractive lady.

"That she is," Giles replied to the banter. "It must be my considerable charm that's so irresistible. Keep in mind, gentleman, she's a very proper lady and guarded by a giant of a man. And the marrying kind, I assure you." He chuckled, raising his hands in mock horror to the idea of marriage.

"Giles, you are smitten! Do not try and have us on. You'll be joining the ranks of those in domestic boredom shortly!" Captain Burns teased while fingering his cards.

A cold glint appeared in Captain Swynford's eyes.

"Aye, she would suit well. Still, I'm young and haven't seen much of the world."

"Then quit the scene and let one of us woo the beauty," another insisted, meaning every word.

"Never. She's mine, lads. I'll have the head of anyone of you who so much as flirts with her!" Giles replied with a hard edge to his voice.

"Don't be so serious, Giles. We are just jealous," Captain Burns cautioned.

Swynford laughed. "Yes, I can see why you might be jealous. Any man would." His face turned very thoughtful, and he leaned back stretching his manly frame in the spindle chair. He suddenly tossed down his cards, scattering them across the table and startling his companions. Running his hand through his thick hair, Giles frowned. His friends glanced at one another and shrugged in bewilderment. Giles was a hard one to understand. He stood abruptly, made his excuses, and left their company.

"A prime example of a man in love," Captain Burns assured his companions. Laughing in unison, they returned to their game.

Katherine did not see Captain Swynford for several days, until he stopped by briefly to tell them Napoleon had left Elba on March first and had reentered Paris on the twentieth. He seemed excited with the surety that he would get his chance to join Wellington at last.

Kate was delighted to see him, but dismayed at the news. She had missed Giles during the last few days. Having easily fallen under his charming spell, she had concluded his absence meant disinterest. Perhaps he had romantic interests elsewhere. Actually, it seemed to her he had been most eager to make her acquaintance, but then had suddenly changed.

Deciding that if there were no other lady, she thought perhaps she had not the town polish or sophistication to hold his attentions. These dreary thoughts led her to seriously consider going to her aunt for a Season, if not to find a husband, then to acquire some experience in the world of London society.

"Miss Spencer, you look like a spring flower," he said as he took a seat in the comfortable family salon. The Spencer home was modest in comparison to the Swynford holdings, but it was nevertheless, a fine Georgian house.

Katherine indeed looked especially pretty in a pale yellow muslin dress trimmed in lace and tied high under her bosom with streamers. The pale yellow created an excellent foil for dark hair.

"Spring is upon us, and it matches my mood," she said lightly.

"A week from tomorrow there is to be a ball in honor of the 'brave' officers, as Mrs. Burnside, who is giving it, so graciously puts it. You would do me an honor to accompany me," he said.

"What a wonderful idea! Yes, I should like to attend very much. I must ask permission from father."

"I've taken the liberty of asking the vicar and his wife to join our party, thus assuring your father's consent," he said, his devilish dimple appearing in his cheek.

"You'll be a formidable opponent to Boney. Obviously, you have a talent for disarming any opposition beforehand," she teased.

"Aye, we northerners think of everything." He chuckled.

Dr. Spencer and Katherine were well thought of but by no means considered part of the local society. Paul Spencer was the fourth son of a well-known country squire. His choice of profession, as well as the death of his beloved Margaret, had removed him from any social scene. However, Captain Swynford had no trouble securing an invitation for Katherine. Mrs. Burnside had indicated she would be delighted to have Katherine as a guest, even if the mothers of unmarried daughters would not. Giles had laughed at the kind lady's tribute to Miss Spencer's good looks.

Katherine explained the coming event to her father at dinner that evening. He readily agreed and was genuinely pleased she would be attending.

"I insist on a new dress," he said.

"We'll have to work swiftly, for it is in a week's time. I want to look my very, very best," Kate said emphatically.

"I wonder why," he teased.

Kate blushed.

"Hmm," her father said thoughtfully.

A dress was fashioned for her by Mrs. Chambers, whose son had been a patient of her father's. Dr. Spencer had saved the boy's arm after a fall from a tree. The dressmaker held the doctor in great respect, and set aside all other work to make Katherine's ball gown.

Katherine requested that it be fashioned of fine cream silk over pale blue. The waist was high, the neck square, and the sleeves were small and puffed. Three tiers of ruffles bound the hemline and these were edged with pale blue silk. The dress fitted Katherine to perfection and showed off her fine neck, shoulders, and bosom. It was discreet, for Katherine was young, but displayed the feminine grace of her figure without being bold.

The night of the ball arrived and there was no doubt in Giles Swynford's eyes when he saw her descend the stairs to greet him. She would be the belle at the ball, and he prided himself on his good luck.

Katherine thought him very handsome in his scarlet coat with its double brass buttons. He certainly was dashing, but it was his light sparkling charm that captivated one, she acknowledged.

"Miss Spencer, I now claim my dances, for when we arrive, I'll need an armed guard to even get near you," he said as he gave an elegant bow.

"Good evening, Captain. You shall have your dances, for who could refuse such a pretty speech?"

"Is that what it is?" he asked.

He took her hand and kissed it lightly. Turning to the Reverend and Mrs. Denniston, he said, "You can now see why I am so pleased you have consented to accompany us."

The kindly vicar smiled. "Good evening, Katherine. You both can be assured that Mrs. Denniston is as pleased as you both are. I'm afraid I'm not the go-about Mrs. Denniston would like. So you see, we are all in agreement."

"Yes, I dearly love an opportunity for some gaiety. My feet don't know they are middle-aged yet. Believe it or not, my husband won my heart with his dancing ability," Mrs. Denniston countered.

"Tut, tut, my dear, I thought it was the sonnets I wrote to you," the vicar said.

Everyone laughed, and Dr. Spencer, who had been observing the happy greetings, thought the vicar would be well served if he added that kind of humor to his sermons. Perhaps he thinks a serious demeanor denotes truth, he thought.

"Mrs. Denniston, you look like a debutante yourself, and I shouldn't wonder but the Reverend Denniston might have to invoke the Almighty's assistance in claiming a dance with you," Dr. Spencer said.

Katherine gave her father an interested look. She seldom saw him in social situations and was surprised by his courtly manner. She wondered, for a fleeting second, what her parents had been like when they were young. Her mother was long dead, and Katherine had not had the opportunity to observe them. But she liked this glimpse of what her father might have been like in his youth. She gave him a warm and loving smile as Dr. Spencer wished them all a pleasant evening.

Captain Swynford assisted Katherine into her velvet cape and took her arm to escort her to the waiting carriage.

Mrs. Burnside greeted her guests in the lower hall of the charming Georgian home. She showed considerable interest in Captain Swynford's lovely companion. Realizing Katherine had grown into quite a beauty, she thought perhaps a match was in the making. It would be an advantageous one for Miss Spencer, for Mrs. Burnside was well aware the Swynfords were a prominent family.

"Thank you for joining us, Miss Spencer," she said.

"It is my pleasure to do so," Katherine replied with a small curtsy.

It is unfortunate she is not well dowered, thought Mrs. Burnside, for then she could reach as high as she might with those striking looks.

"Do enjoy your evening," Mrs. Burnside said as she turned, smiling, to her next guest.

Katherine entered the ballroom on Giles's arm. The room had been draped with regimental flags and red and white flowers stood in large baskets. The flames of at least a thousand candles gave off a warm glow and the sounds of laughter and music rose over the charming scene. Bejeweled ladies, all wearing their very best ball gowns because such occasions were not frequent in Dover, mingled among dashing scarlet-coated gentlemen.

"How lovely!" Katherine exclaimed.

"Aye, that you are." Giles laughed, intentionally misunderstanding her remark.

"You know how to raise a lady's spirits, Captain," she said with an exaggerated bat of her eyelashes.

Captain Swynford laughed. "You learn fast."

They made a handsome pair as he led her to the dance

floor. Kate had been taught to dance but had had little opportunity to execute what she had learned. Giles was a superb dancer and led her expertly through the steps. She managed quite well. The young men who watched were not contemplating her dancing skills, however, but figuring how soon they might secure a dance on her card.

She smiled at Giles with a happiness that added to her glow.

They were besieged by every acquaintance of Captain Swynford's for an introduction. Soon Katherine found herself surrounded by scarlet-coated officers all vying for a dance. She was a success and she loved every minute of it. Not once did she sit out a dance. Many a matron looked at their overshadowed daughters in dismay, thinking it was a good thing Miss Spencer was not a part of the *beau monde*. However, it seemed that might change now, and so many hoped that Katherine would marry soon.

Giles had claimed the supper dance and therefore escorted her in to dine with several of his friends and their ladies. The young people laughed and teased each other and the mood was gay despite the many references to coming battles with Napoleon. Though Katherine was not shy, she sat quietly listening to the flow of talk, happy just to observe the others.

When they returned to the ballroom, Captain Burns, a colleague of Giles's, asked her to dance. "I can see why Giles is so enchanted, Miss Spencer," he said as he led her through a country set.

"Indeed? And why is that?" she teased.

"Ah ha, you want me to tell you how taken he is," he answered.

"No, Captain, I'll allow him that privilege," she replied, looking up to him in feigned wide-eyed innocence.

Captain Burns chuckled. "Lucky man, I'd say."

They finished the dance and he escorted her back to Giles.

Katherine and Giles had the last dance and she suspected he was a bit in his cups. He was very solicitous but that slight remote demeanor had returned. It must be because they are off to war, Katherine thought. She made every effort to be as lighthearted and amusing as possible.

The carriage ride home was quiet, for all the occupants were tired from the evening's festivities. Captain Swynford thanked the vicar and his wife for their kind assistance and said he should like to walk back to the barracks.

"Good night, Katherine, it was a pleasure for us all," Mrs. Denniston said as they waved their farewells and the carriage moved away.

Giles took her arm and walked her to the door. "As always, I am in your debt. Thank you, Miss Spencer, for the most wonderful evening. I suspect it will not be long before we leave, but I'll carry the memory of this evening with me when I depart." He bent to kiss her hand.

"Thank you, Captain. I could not have enjoyed myself more. We all will hold you in our prayers for a safe return. Soon perhaps, it will all be over."

"Aye, that it will," he solemnly answered. "Good night," he said as her front door was opened by Dr. Spencer. "I'll call before I leave." He turned to walk down the dark street.

In early April, Giles called upon Katherine once more and requested to speak with her. He felt fortunate that she did not always have a female in attendance as most of his acquaintances were required to do. Wearing a cream muslin dress with a short rose spencer, she entered the salon and greeted him with a heart-warming smile. He crossed the small room quickly with both arms outstretched and took her hands in his own. He squeezed her fingers and his light brown eyes intently searched her upturned face.

"Katherine, I have my orders! We leave next tide to join Wellington. It looks as though Boney has not had his last battle. Wish me well!"

He took her into his arms and kissed her quickly, paused, and kissed her again.

Katherine was surprised but offered no resistance, when his lips touched hers. She closed her eyes, enjoying the feel of his strong arms around her. Her pulse quickened as she thrilled to her first kiss from a man.

He cupped her chin in his hand and stood silently for a moment, then gently put her from him. "I'll write," he said as he moved to take his leave.

After he had gone, Katherine stood in the middle of the room for some minutes. Her hand went to her lips. So, she thought, that is what it feels like to be kissed. It certainly was pleasant, she thought, blushing. Yet she was perplexed. Why had he not come often of late? And why had he offered what was considered a declaration of intention and yet made no other offer than that he would write? She stood silent and thought of her reaction to his kisses. They had pleased her. She flushed and hoped he would write to her as he had promised.

Suddenly, all was justified in her mind. It was the war, she thought. Indeed, he was probably being noble and very honest, for battle guaranteed no return. Tears stung her eyes, as it occurred to her that she might never see him again.

Chapter 4

Katherine received two letters from Captain Swynford. The first arrived the early days of spring, and expressed Giles's high spirits and his eager anticipation of his joining Wellington's forces. He wrote that he was proud to be a line officer and hoped to be worthy of the responsibility. He told her he had purchased her a silver cross on one of his sightseeing excursions and would bring it back to her. The letter glowingly described a succession of parades and watering orders and field days in which he had taken part, and told how deficiencies in blankets and arms had been made good.

The second letter was full of the accounts of Wellington's retreats, forced by the French commander, Marshal Michel Ney. Giles's enthusiastic tone was now gone, for he told of the death and destruction he had seen on the retreat from Quatre Bras to Mont St. Jean. He wrote that the wind and rain had been beyond anything he had seen and described how the horses and carts bogged down in the mire among the scattered dead.

In the letter, Giles wrote that Napoleon had been seen on his white mare, Désirée, by the rear guard of the Brunswick infantry as they retreated to Mont St. Jean. They now camped around the village of Waterloo, in Belgium. He was not sure this letter would reach her but he wanted her to know he was well and thought of her often, and could hardly wait until he returned.

Katherine clasped the letter to her chest in relief, having heard news of the Battle of Waterloo several days before she received Giles's second letter. The British victory gave her a false sense of his well-being and she felt a surge of joy as she thought of his safe return.

All England rejoiced at the news of Wellington's victory of Napoleon. In every city and village, church bells rang out, proclaiming the long-awaited end to the hostilities. Though Napoleon had led the French army into battle himself, the Prussian forces, led by Marshal Gebhard von Blucher, had combined with British and Allied troops to crush the French, bringing the Napoleonic era to a close. Elation ran through the English people at fever pitch, as the war had long caused them great sacrifice.

Dr. Spencer joined in the celebration of the end of the war, but braced himself against the onslaught of casualties that would enter Dover, and other British ports. There was no consolation in the fact that at least these would not be the worst. The worst, he knew, would not make it home. He also realized that he would, once more, need Katherine's help. As he remembered Captain Swynford's shock at learning that Katherine assisted him in surgery, his conscience once again pricked him, and he vowed to send her to London in September.

In early July, Dr. Spencer received a letter informing him that a Captain Swynford was en route to Dover and sought his service, as he had been badly wounded. Though he was being cared for by two of his faithful soldiers, it was somewhat doubtful, whether he would make it to port alive.

He hurried out to the small back garden where

Katherine was sitting on a stone bench. It was a beautiful clear day and the sun lit the profusion of flowers while bees hummed softly as they busied themselves among the roses and delphiniums around her. Lazily sitting with a book resting on her lap, Katherine looked up to see her father approaching her, a drawn look upon his face and a letter in his hand.

"Father, what is amiss? I see it plainly written on your face," she said, rising from her seat.

" 'Tis best you sit, for I have sad news," he replied uncertainly. He was not sure what, if any, attachment she might have for the young captain.

"I have just received news that Captain Swynford was wounded at Waterloo and is being escorted here to Dover," he said as he handed her the missive. Watching the changes on her face as she read the letter, he supposed her feelings for the captain might be considerable.

"Father, I cannot believe it! God willing, let us hope the wound is not too grave!" she cried, tears streaming down her cheeks.

Though he had expected her to be upset, Dr. Spencer was taken back by the force of her response.

"We must find him as soon as he arrives . . ." Her voice trailed off.

"Do you wish me to bring him here, Katherine? We could take far better care of him than the hospitals the army has set up. I think that is the intention of the letter," he said softly, sitting down next to her. He placed a loving arm about her shoulder.

"Oh, indeed, there is no other choice. We can do far more for him in our home. I pray he is not too badly wounded, though the letter gives no such assurance," she replied as she leaned her head on her father's shoulder.

"I shall comb the rosters and bring him here as soon as he arrives. Please, do not fret. We will do all that is possible.'' He patted her hand. He was worried at the news of Giles's injury but now also by Katherine's obvious concern.

Early each morning Dr. Spencer left the house to meet every incoming vessel, looking for Captain Swynford. His search was not long since the wounded Captain arrived only three days after the letter.

Dr. Spencer found Giles aboard the naval warship *Warrior.* The smell of putrid flesh had assailed his senses as he searched among amputees, men on stretchers, and walking wounded with grave, haunted faces. His compassion overwhelmed him as he viewed the damage done to so many. He could not bring himself to believe that such carnage could ever be justified.

His search was finally rewarded when he found Captain Swynford in a tiny, dark cabin attended by two faithful comrades. Dr. Spencer quickly introduced himself.

"I am Dr. Spencer, come to fetch Captain Swynford," he said gravely, his eyes traveling to the pale young man lying motionless upon the cot.

"The trip has done him no good, to be sure," replied a short ruddy-complexioned man. He extended his hand. "Captain Downs, and this is Lieutenant Bradshaw."

Dr. Spencer acknowledged the introduction with quick, perfunctory handshakes, then stepping over to the bedside of the prone man, he made a swift appraisal of his wounds.

Dr. Spencer shook his head. "I will not waste time now. We must carefully move him to my home at once," he said, his voice betraying none of his shock and foreboding at seeing Giles's condition. He knew the captain might not even survive the transfer from the ship to the bed he had waiting.

Dr. Spencer sent Lieutenant Bradshaw to procure a

cart and Captain Downs to fetch a stretcher. A soft moan escaped the wounded man's lips and Dr. Spencer noted the fresh blood oozing from his rough bandages. God, let me get him home, he prayed.

Carefully, they threaded their way through the ship down to the docks, where they laid Giles in the cart. While the doctor and Lieutenant Bradshaw tended the patient in the back, Captain Downs drove the cart through the streets. Finally, they arrived at the Spencer home, where, with the help of Norton, the wounded soldier was lifted gently into a waiting bed.

The move had brought even a whiter pallor to Captain Swynford's face and a blueness about his lips. Dr. Spencer worked with dispatch, washing and examining the deep wounds in Giles's chest and left arm. He was relieved to see no signs of gangrene. After dressing the wound with fresh bandages, he tried to make the patient as comfortable as possible, for he knew the young man desperately needed rest and could not endure more probing.

Dr. Spencer had not allowed Katherine to assist, hoping to keep her from knowing of the extent of the captain's wounds. There would be more than enough time for her to help, Dr. Spencer thought, for he knew it would be a very long recovery.

Captain Swynford clung tenaciously to life. After he survived the first critical night, a routine was set for his care, allowing Dr. Spencer to return to the care of his many other patients. Giles's nursing was left primarily to Kate and Norton, who took turns sitting with the patient. The other household servants lent whatever help they could. Mrs. Powell prepared strengthening broths that were spoon-fed to the captain in his lucid moments. Daniels, the groom, helped Norton bathe him and lift him to change the bed linens.

Dr. Spencer was gratified with Giles's progress, for he had not thought Captain Swynford would live through the first night. Paul Spencer sensed in the young captain a strong will as he determinedly fought for his life.

On the fourth day after his arrival in Dover, Katherine sat quietly beside Giles in the sunny room. As she watched him peacefully sleeping, she pondered the first dreadful day that he had arrived. Captain Swynford had been in constant pain and cried out often in delirium. Those cries had sent a knife through her heart. Her anguish at his agony had compelled her to spend many long hours at his side.

Now she smiled to see he had found a restful sleep at last. It seemed to her his color was even better. Closing her eyes, she said a fervent prayer of thanks for this slight improvement.

Her growing anxiety over Captain Swynford's condition had not escaped the notice of her father. He had, on several occasions, insisted that she leave the captain's side to get the rest she herself needed. He wondered about her attachment to the young man, and worried that she had confused her compassion for the young man with affection. But there was nothing he could do about this, for Katherine was totally devoted to the captain's welfare. He decided he had to trust his daughter's sensible character.

As Giles moved slightly, Katherine's eyes flew to his face. She reached over to touch his hand.

"Lucinda?" he whispered the name so softly, it was almost inaudible.

Katherine withdrew her hand and sat back with a perplexed frown. Who was Lucinda? Was she someone he had a *tendre* for or perhaps was even engaged to?

"No, Captain, it is Katherine Spencer," she replied quietly, feeling a slight sinking in the pit of her stomach.

His eyes fluttered open, and stared at her unseeing. Slowly, realization dawned in his eyes. "Where am I?" he asked.

"Here in Dover with Dr. Spencer and myself."

He turned his head and gave her the sweetest smile she had ever seen. "Are you sure I'm not in heaven with an angel by my side?" he teased weakly. "How did I come to be here?"

"Captain Downs and Lieutenant Bradshaw brought you to us. You have been recovering from your wounds, Captain Swynford. We are delighted at your considerable progress." She smiled down at him.

He watched her for a moment. Lord, he thought, she is a beauty. "You are an angel of mercy, and the most beautiful one a poor soldier could have," he sighed. He closed his eyes, drifting once more into slumber.

A slight flush rose into her cheeks, and she lowered her eyes. She toyed with her fingers in confusion. It's just a pretty manner of speech, she thought, but found herself hoping that he had meant the compliment.

Captain Swynford continued to improve after this first moment of lucid consciousness. The routine of his care continued. Katherine now spent hours reading and visiting with him. He began to speak of his Northumberland home with longing.

One day, he was slightly propped up on pillows, his wounded arm still in a sling. The room was cheerful and sunny and the midmorning light showed that healthy color had returned to his skin. Katherine thought he looked very romantic and decided to tease him.

"Captain, you languish so gracefully, all Lord Bryon's devotees would desert him if they could but see you."

"If I could charm you as well, then I should feign helplessness just to keep you by my side," he replied. The appearance of the merry twinkle in his eyes warmed Katherine's heart. She chuckled.

He watched her silently for a moment as if contemplating something. She waited, knowing he was on the brink of speaking seriously.

"Katherine, you would love the wild beauty of the

north," he said. She was a bit taken aback since she had expected him to speak of some other topic, but she sensed an anxiousness in him and waited expectantly.

"The hills there are covered with heather. The blue purple of the hills and the wild expanse of the fields all would enchant you. You can ride out for miles. The wind is slightly tangy with the sea air that wafts in gently from the shore. Oh, you would love it so, I know," he said with sparkling eyes.

"Indeed, how could anyone not love what you have described." She laughed. "You convince me, I promise."

"No, it is more than that. I can't explain, but I look into your brilliant blue eyes and know you belong there." His voice was as soft as a caress and carried an undisguised intimacy.

She looked into his light gold-brown eyes, intrigued by the intensity she saw in them.

"Come with me to Marston Hall. Take me home, Katherine . . . Please take me home. If I am to die . . . I wish to die there."

Katherine's heart leaped and her temples pounded with a rush of blood. "Captain Swynford! You are not going to die. Why, each day you are better. It will take time, of course. . . ." Her words trailed off as tears filled her eyes and she reached out to take his hand.

He raised her fingers to his lips. "For God's sake, call me Giles, and answer my proposal . . . now."

A tingle ran down her spine, and her heart gave another lurch. How should she answer him, she wondered.

"I do not know what to say. I . . ." she confessed, a sweet, compassionate expression lighting her oval face.

Giles Swynford recognized her sympathy, and since he always had been able to capitalize on any vulnerability he perceived in others, he seized this opportunity.

"Katherine, I am asking you to marry me. Marry me and accompany me home. I need you," he persisted.

She sat quietly with her hand still in his. She knew her regard for him had grown with each passing day. He was so handsome and charming, she reasoned. Who would not be taken with him? Did she love him? Did she know what love was? Still, it was with eagerness that her footsteps carried her to his bedside each morning.

"I must consider this, Giles. Marriage is so . . . permanent. I would want to be sure." She hesitated, yet at the same time, her heart went out to him.

"Katherine, my angel of mercy, I can make you happy. I know my recovery will prevent me from riding the moors with you for a while, but we will—with the wind in our faces. You belong there, with me. You are not indifferent to me, I know," he said in all sincerity. "Come with me, take me home."

The thought of not being with Giles filled her with loneliness. She had grown so used to having him in her thoughts and care that her only answer could be to consent.

"Yes, Giles, I shall marry you. How can I refuse such charm?" She laughed and bent over to kiss him on his cheek.

He reached for her with his right arm and stroked her cheek with his hand. "Thank you, angel. You'll not regret it, I promise."

Chapter 5

The gray gloom of early morning seeped into the room just as the early autumn chill penetrated her bones. It took her a moment to recall where she was since a gray fog seemed to linger in her mind. Weary, she was so weary. She opened her eyes to the austere, whitewashed walls of the small gabled room.

Katherine lay on her cot next to Giles's bed and listened to the labored breathing of her husband. The cold dampness of the early autumn air was certainly detrimental to his progress, she thought. In fact, he seemed to fail a little each day. She closed her eyes in pain of that thought.

Dear God, she prayed, allow me to get him home where he can truly mend. She knew it was his fierce determination to reach Marston Hall that compelled him to withstand the pain and agonies of this seemingly endless journey. It had now become her own crusade. However, since they had been forced to stop in the small country inn and rest for several days so Giles could regain strength, she began to doubt they would ever finish it. Tears welled in her eyes. Seeing Giles grit his teeth against the pain, while he constantly pressed for the continuation of the journey, and all the while watching his health fail was taking a toll on her. She knew her own strength was ebbing and she must use this respite to gather her own forces.

She thought of her father, and how he had grudgingly consented to her marriage. How well she could remember his reluctance when Giles had asked his permission. Later, Paul Spencer had called her into his study to caution her. She could still hear his words.

"Katherine, you take a great task that may well leave you a widow. You have never experienced the parties and balls in London, and for that I fault myself. Are you certain you really wish to marry Giles? You actually know little of him," he had said as his blue eyes clouded with worry.

Katherine had sat quietly in the comfortable study, doubt surging in her own breast at his words. But she had answered in the affirmative.

"Yes, Father, it is what I wish. He needs me. He is certainly all that is charm, and will make a most admirable husband. I am exceedingly fond of him," she had said, lowering her eyes. Her own doubt was quickly quelled when she imagined Giles recovered, laughing and teasing her as was his way. She smiled at this thought.

Dr. Spencer interpreted her smile to mean she genuinely desired to wed Giles.

"So be it," he replied with a pang of regret. "Remember, you may always return home if all does not go well with the journey. Giles will not listen to my advice to remain until he is fully recovered." Dr. Spencer shook his head in sad resignation. He knew the greater part of his reluctance was due to the fact he must part with Katherine. He would miss her sorely, but she must have a chance for her own life. He had protected her far too long.

Remembering that conversation, Katherine now tossed on the small cot set up next to Giles's bed. Her thoughts still lingered in Dover, where they had been quietly married at Giles's bedside. She remembered her soft cream dress trimmed in Belgian lace and how suddenly her fears had faded when Giles looked at her. The admiration shining from his eyes as he reached to take her hand had swept away all doubt.

"No man ever had a more beautiful bride. My family will adore you!" He smiled his sweetest smile and her heart had melted.

Careful steps had been taken to ensure Giles's comfort during the journey. One seat of the large traveling carriage was made into a bed for him. The carriage traveled slowly as speed had to be sacrificed for comfort. Katherine had regretted that fact, for time was important. Though their pace was not swift, their carriage had jostled somewhat and it had not been good for Giles. Still, he had gritted his teeth and demanded that they continue.

They now rested in an inn called the Angel and Royal, which had a lovely fifteenth-century stone front and faced the marketplace in the village of Grantham. They were over halfway to Northumberland, and hoped their journey would soon be over.

Giles's restless movements brought Katherine's thoughts back to the present. Dr. Putney, the local doctor, had seemed competent and she had been grateful for his emphatic advice that they remain at the inn for at least a fortnight. If not, he had insisted, he could not guarantee their safe arrival in Northumberland. Katherine sensed in the kindly doctor's words the unspoken opinion that safe arrival would be dubious in any event. He had not said so directly but his insistence on recovery time before continuance of their journey had made it very plain the outcome was gravely in question.

Katherine gazed at the whitewashed walls of their small bedchamber and sighed. Giles, she knew, would be more comfortable at Marston Hall, and surely his recovery would be swifter there. Stretching her arms, for the cot offered little comfort and her back ached, she continued to dwell on their strange odyssey.

The burning determination that shone from Giles's feverish eyes somehow still gave her hope they would make it. There was some kind of unspoken pact that if they could just reach Marston Hall, all would be well. Giles believed it so strongly he had withstood the agonies of the journey this far. She began to believe it as fervently as he.

But Marston Hall was an unknown entity to Katherine, and she wondered how she would be received. Certainly his family did not even know Giles had married. Would they accept her gladly? She had not understood Giles's reluctance to write his family of his marriage and return, let alone his wounds. They had argued over it, but in the end she had acceded to Giles's will, though she did not understand or agree with him.

Katherine tossed a little in bed as she contemplated the new family that was soon to be hers. God only knows, she thought, they should be ever grateful for her care and effort to return a beloved family member to them.

The sounds of servants stirring in the inn brought Katherine's mind back to the realities of this new day, and she rose quickly to attend Giles. He was still sleeping; she silently reached to feel his brow, thinking perhaps the fever had abated during the night. His color even appeared to be a bit better. She was gratified to feel his forehead was cool and dry, and hurried to begin the day.

Katherine placed some coals on the embers in the grate in hopes of warding off the damp and chilly air. Quickly removing her nightgown, she washed in the cool water remaining in the basin. She shivered. Autumn is upon us, she thought, and the cold does Giles no good. We must hurry. She donned the warm serviceable wool gown that had been her mainstay since leaving Dover.

Strange, she thought as she dressed, how she had come to accept the role of Giles's wife even with its unusual circumstances, and could execute her toilette in the same room with him without the slightest embarrassment. One could adapt to any circumstances no matter how odd or difficult, she mused. Certainly she and Giles had become the best of friends, though they had never been lovers.

She had just finished plaiting her hair into a braid and wrapping it on top of her head when the innkeeper's robust wife knocked and entered carrying a tray of hot bread, ham, and tea. "Good morning, my lady. How be your husband this day?" she asked, casting a look toward the bed where the wounded Giles slept.

"He seemed to sleep more restfully than he has for many a night. Please bring some warm water so that I can bathe him and ask if Norton will come to help me change his nightdress. Dr. Putney will be here to change his dressings and I want him as comfortable as possible," Katherine replied.

"Aye, my lady, but sit yourself here first and take a bit of breakfast," the innkeeper's wife said with kindness as she placed the tray on the small table.

Katherine obeyed and found the tea warmed her through, giving a lift to her spirits. The food, likewise, tasted delicious and she ate more than she had in days. Renewed hope glimmered in her heart, as she felt her strength return.

Shortly afterwards, Norton lumbered in wearing a cheerful grin. The evening's rest had likewise done much to relieve his weariness.

"Is he better, Miss Kate?" he asked, moving toward the bed to help Katherine. She nodded.

Working together, they carefully stripped off Giles's nightshirt. Katherine sighed in relief, for she could see no fresh blood. Norton nodded his approval as he gently lowered the young man back onto the bed. Giles stirred and allowed a soft moan to escape his lips.

Katherine had to admit he was a marvelously handsome man. Even in illness he looked only like a wounded Sir Galahad. Katherine giggled softly at her fancy. What a silly idea, she thought. But he was finely featured and strongly built and she would have to be blind not to admire him.

Norton glanced curiously at his mistress, wondering at the merriment that had just escaped her lips. He did not approve of this hasty marriage and foolish trek across the country. Still, he thought, if the young captain didn't die, he would surely make a good husband and take good care of Katherine, for he seemed a fine young gentleman.

Norton never doubted for a moment that the captain was dependable. But he was glad Miss Katherine had himself to depend on, as she had since her leading-string days. Harold Norton could always be counted on to take care of Miss Kate. He shook his head at the possibility of Giles's dying and Miss Kate being left alone. Well, for now she had a husband, he thought, albeit a gravely wounded one, and himself to look after her until the young captain recovered.

Norton took the dirty bed linens out to be washed and said he would be back shortly. As he left, Katherine said a prayer of gratitude for Norton. She knew she would have been helpless without him. Thank God her father had not allowed her to make the journey without this kind man's assistance.

When Dr. Putney arrived he gravely announced a slight improvement in the patient and proceeded to change his dressings. He was relieved, as Katherine had been, to see the wound had no fresh blood and emphatically reiterated the importance of delaying their journey so Giles could rest. As long as he was not moved for two weeks, the captain just might make the arduous journey to Northumberland.

Each day, Katherine kept watch over the bed of her husband. Norton often relieved her so that she could rest or get some exercise. She took long walks along the village road during midday when the thin warmth of the sun shone down through the trees. The combination of rest, good food and long walks in the fresh air brought back her natural bloom. The villagers came to recognize her and regarded her kindly as the story of the brave lady who was taking her wounded hero husband home became general knowledge.

There was no doubt that Giles made daily improvement, however slight. While still too weak to stand or walk, he was lucid and his humor began to return. His gold-brown eyes twinkled as he teased Katherine. "Kate, how does it feel to be nursemaid to an errant warrior? I know you must be perishing from boredom."

"Why, Sir Knight, I am honored to assist a hero of Waterloo. I'm admired whenever I venture out. Did you know this inn was once a hostelry of the Knights Templar? The innkeeper is very proud of that fact. So you see, you fit their clientele very well," she answered.

"You see me as a shining knight? Hardly. Still, you may be quite accurate in your opinion." He laughed and saluted her smartly with his right hand. "Speaking of warriors, Kate, we may make it to Marston with me still alive. How Richard Coeur-de-lion will hate it. He is an ogre, for he will have all doing his bidding only."

"The lion-hearted, you call him the lion-hearted? Why? It was you who have braved the battlefield, not he! He isn't braver than you, he only played the father to you. I can't wait till he sees how well you are. Of course, he doesn't even know you're wounded."

"He knows."

"How so, when you have forbidden my writing to him?" she asked.

"He will know and he will hate it!" Giles replied, a naughty gleam in his eyes.

"Will he hate me, Giles, or the fact that you have married without his consent?" she asked.

The teasing light faded from his eyes and he suddenly turned his head away.

"Is something wrong, Giles? Will he not really approve of me?" she asked.

Turning to face her, he replied, "He will approve and think you beautiful, as truly you are. Pay no mind to me, angel. We will manage quite well."

"Giles, how does what I look like signify? What has that to do with liking a person? God forbid that should ever be so. What kind of person would only like another for his appearance?"

Giles closed his eyes as if to sleep, but Katherine felt he was only avoiding her questions. Just what was his brother the marquess like? Could he indeed be so formidable that he would make the fact he had no say in choosing Giles's bride a factor in accepting her? He had best understand it was she and Norton who even achieved Giles's safe return.

Katherine shrugged. She did not care a fig what the marquess did or did not think.

Within ten days Giles was better and complaining bitterly that they must continue the journey. Dr. Putney was as reluctant to grant their departure as Paul Spencer had been when they left Dover. He did agree that his patient was much improved, but his wound was deep and not totally healed.

"He should not be bounced about in a traveling carriage. It is sheer folly not to allow his wounds to heal completely," Dr. Putney warned. It was to no avail, though, for Giles Swynford insisted on returning home immediately.

So they made plans to resume their journey. Giles was concerned that they would not have sufficient money because the trip was taking many days longer than expected. Katherine offered to sell her pearl earrings. She was slightly annoyed that he did not demur, but instead loudly declared he would buy her a new pair, twice as large, once they reached home. Kate lowered her eyes lest her hurt show. Home, was Marston Hall that? Her earrings were one of a few possessions she had in memory of her mother and her own home.

Dismissing such thoughts as childish, she donned her heavy cape and walked the short distance to the only goldsmith in the village. She sold the earrings for far less than their value, she knew, but she had no choice.

Katherine and Norton readied the carriage for their departure. The weather had turned cooler, and they bundled Giles in blankets on the seat, making him as comfortable as possible.

"Kate, you'll have me cosseted like a babe." He laughed, but a slight drawn line quivered about his mouth. Katherine shut her eyes against the tears that threatened to flow at his expression. He had showed he was still in great pain when they moved him, and despite their very careful effort, the task had been a nightmare.

"We'll cosset you all the way to Marston Hall. Then you can lead a charge over the moat, or whatever you wish. I assume the marquess would not be without a moat!" she teased.

"Indeed not, and a dungeon too, Kate, you will find the manor all I have said it to be," he sighed. It would be good to get home, he thought with determination. He had to explain himself to Lucinda . . .

Katherine knew the journey was just too much for Giles. Norton also began to feel apprehension, since it was he who carried the wounded man from the carriage to whatever beds might have been secured for the night. Norton could see how much pain Giles was in. Inns varied from one to another. Still, Giles was now even more adamant that they continue on.

"Giles, you did so much better when we rested. Let us do so again," Kate begged.

"Kate, do not worry. I know it is tiring but we must get on. I have wasted too much time. Take me home, Kate, as quickly as you can."

She had no answer to that. How could she plead more than she had? Perhaps he was correct. The more quickly they ended the journey, the sooner her husband could begin to truly mend.

The days and nights followed in worried monotony, one after the other. The passing terrain changed but the occupants of the cumbersome traveling coach paid little heed to the scenery. Giles was still in pain and Katherine administered laudanum to him, as directed, so that he would sleep and not be so keenly aware of the rough roads.

She thought she would go mad. This was the most idiotic venture ever attempted. Giles should have remained in Dover. Still, he persisted.

"Kate," he whispered, "we are so near to home. It's as if I can smell the sea. You've done this for me and I'm grateful." He reached for her hand.

Kate glanced at Norton and saw the worry in his eyes. When she looked back at Giles, he had closed his eyes again.

Chapter 6

Giles knew they would make Marston Hall by late afternoon. His recent trials and pain seemed to fade from his mind as a feeling of joy and optimism filled him. All will be right now, he thought. His excitement and anticipation infused energy into the countenance of his companions.

They were passing through Alnwick, a village just a few hours south of Marston Hall and Giles rallied. "Alnwick was a great stronghold against the Scots," he told Kate in an excited voice. "Alnwick Castle, which belonged to the Duke of Northumberland, had stood under the Percys as guard against the Scots. The castle still boasts stone sentries which silently gaze from the battlements, put there, long ago, to deceive invading Scots." He chuckled softly. "We northerners are known for toughness as well as duplicity. Below the castle there are still the ruins of a monastery, beyond that the sea. I shall take you there someday. You will be fascinated."

Katherine turned to face him and smiled at his obvious happiness. She leaned her head back and closed her eyes for a moment. We have done what was almost impossible, she thought. He heart leaped in anticipation and relief; she was pleased that the journey seemed almost completed.

They passed through the old stone gates of Alnwick village with its carved lions guarding the bridge.

"In less than two hours, we shall be home," Giles sighed as if all else was of no importance.

And so it was, as the sun glowed red in the late afternoon, that their carriage turned into a lane between ivy-covered walls boasting the same type of ferocious feline guards as were seen at Alnwick. The manor was set well back on a high knoll, and Katherine was surprised to see it had an extensive park. The late sun's rays cast a fiery glow upon the colored stone of the magnificent manor. Marston Hall was monumental and Katherine was overwhelmed by its enormous size.

The carriage passed through a huge archway into a courtyard. It was obvious that at one time this had been a fortress as well as the Swynford family seat. They halted in front of two large oak doors and the coachman swung down to assist the travelers.

One huge oak door opened and a tall, thin butler accompanied by two liveried footmen hurried to the waiting coach.

" 'Tis Master Giles returned to us!" the butler cried with uncharacteristic enthusiasm, for he usually held the distant reserve of his lofty position in the household.

Mrs. Dodd, the housekeeper, squealed with delight, her ample bosom heaving in excitement. "Faith be preserved, we knew not of your coming," she cried out in equal enthusiasm as she scampered down the step to lend assistance.

A hush fell over the delighted servants as they realized Giles was ill. They watched in silence as Norton's hulking frame gently lifted Captain Swynford from the carriage.

Mrs. Dodd was sent flying, calling orders to ready Master Giles's bedchamber. Her face showed her annoyance that they had not sent word ahead of their arrival so that she could have had all prepared.

It was some minutes before Giles was carefully laid in his bed. A fire had already been lit to warm the room and tea called for.

Word of Giles's injury spread quickly through the hall and the faithful servants expressed their shock and dismay.

"Aye, it was at the Battle of Waterloo that the young master received his wounds," Latimer, the butler, explained in a whisper to each and every servant that came hurriedly to the front hall upon hearing of Captain Swynford's arrival.

Resting back on his pillow, Giles thought only that he was home at last. He closed his eyes a moment to savor their successful journey. The gathered servants stood silent and dismayed, glancing to one another in helpless concern.

"Latimer, Mrs. Dodd, may I present my wife, Katherine Swynford." He smiled up under veiled eyes to watch their reaction.

All eyes turned to Katherine in utter surprise. She blushed at their obvious scrutiny.

She had dressed with care that morning, knowing they would reach Marston Hall before dark. She had chosen a soft blue traveling dress and pelisse trimmed in black soutage braid which perfectly complimented her black hair and brilliant blue eyes. However, she felt tired and rumpled from the journey, though her beauty was obvious to all who stood gaping at her.

She smiled ever so tentatively. "We are pleased to return my husband to his home in order that he recover. It was his wish to do so," she said formally with a creeping feeling of unease.

"Without Kate and Norton, I would not have accomplished this feat. I am ever grateful to them, for it was no easy task," Giles said with some force.

Katherine continued to be embarrassed as the servants stared at her in unabashed interest. Self-consciously, she removed her bonnet and cloak and handed it to the footman standing near the door.

"Where is Richard? Surely he would welcome his long-absent brother," Giles said with an edge of rancor. Tiring, he closed his eyes to shut out the pain that consumed his body.

"His Lordship is not at home. We expect his return in a day or so," answered Latimer in his usual formal voice. He cast an uneasy glance to Mrs. Dodd.

A dark flush of anger crossed Giles's face. "Well, no matter, he will have plenty of time to enjoy the pleasure of my bride's and my own company," he bitterly uttered before he drifted into unconsciousness.

Neither Latimer nor Mrs. Dodd wished to inform Giles that Lord Marston had escorted his wife's body back to Dunston to be buried, at her father's request, in her family's vault.

" 'Tis a sad day," whispered Mrs. Dodd to Latimer when they left the room. "For he knows not of Lady Lucinda's death."

Latimer had dismissed each servant with a task. Separate bedchambers were prepared for Katherine and Norton. She was given a chamber near Giles but insisted that a cot for her be placed in the dressing room adjacent to Giles's room. "I shall sleep near my husband in order to nurse him as long as needed," she declared.

After some warm broth and an excellent dinner in her room, Katherine quickly washed herself from a small basin and donned a nightdress which the chambermaid had unpacked from her valise. She had decided to sleep in the dressing room while Norton assumed the first sick watch. She would later relieve him so that he might rest also.

Katherine took down her dark hair and brushed it as the fire cast dancing shadows about the room. She began to relax as the warmth from the grate flooded her body. When she crawled into the small bed it was but minutes before she slept.

It was just past midnight when a carriage, drawn by four perfectly matched grays, entered the courtyard. The sound of the clacking horses' hooves and the wheels rattling on the stone broke the stillness of the night. Above, the sky was clear and cold. The pale silvery moonlight had allowed Lord Marston to press the coachman to reach Marston Hall without stopping at some inferior inn.

Richard Swynford was tired. The past week had been fraught with emotion, but at least it was over. Lucinda's mother, Lady Rawlins, had carried on like a banshee, and while Richard could sympathize, he himself had felt nothing but regret. His marriage had been a disaster, and Lady Rawlins had made it apparent she held Richard responsible for her daughter's untimely death. Shrugging off this thought, Lord Marston alighted from the coach.

The Marquess of Marston was a tall, finely built man who moved with a sense of purpose. He stepped down from the coach just as one heavy oak door flew open to reveal Latimer waiting with a taper to light his way.

"Good evening, Latimer. It is late I know, but bring me some brandy, for I am weary beyond measure," he said as he pushed past Latimer.

"Your lordship, Master Giles is home! He was wounded at Waterloo, and he—" Latimer broke off as Lord Marston turned sharply around, his seven-caped coat twirling about him.

"Where is he?" he demanded, his face matching his harsh tone.

"We have put him in his own chamber. He is seriously injured, and I fear—"

"Put my brandy in my chamber. I go to Giles, now!" Lord Marston's low resonant voice echoed in the hall. He mounted the staircase, taking the steps two at a time.

Latimer tried unsuccessfully to keep up with the Marquess. "Your lordship, he has brought—"

"Never mind that, get Robbins and my brandy, now!" Richard called over his shoulder.

Lord Marston's cold hazel-green eyes sparkled with fire and his handsome face was set in a strong frown as he strode down to his brother's room.

Katherine was awakened by the sound of voices. She lay still a moment, trying to recollect just where she was. Had the voices come from outside or from Giles's room? She jumped out of bed, thinking that Giles might have called to her. Did he need her? Creaking open the heavy door, she quietly walked to the bed only to find Giles unmoving and apparently sound asleep. On the other side of the huge bed, Norton lowered his eyes, for he did not wish to call attention to her nightdress.

She smiled at him. "Go get some rest. I am wide-awake now. Go, for I'll need your help in the morning."

"Yes, missy, I'll not argue with ye. My old bones ache for sleep. Summon me if ye need me." He rose slowly, placing his huge hands upon his knees and wearily pushing himself up. Katherine watched with sympathy. Norton glanced at Giles, nodded in approval, and lumbered from the room.

Katherine ran her hands through her tumbling mass of dark curls. Her thin nightdress did little to ward off early autumn's chill, despite the fine fire Norton had kept burning in the fireplace. She must go fetch her robe and slippers, she thought as she leaned over the bed to feel Giles's forehead.

Just then, the chamber door flew open, and a cool rush of air swirled around the room. Loud footsteps came toward her, echoing in the chamber. The bed dressings prevented her view of the entrance but the firelight cast a shadow that grew larger and larger on the wall, crossing the ceiling, as the steps drew nearer. Her heart began to pound in her chest. Slowly, she straightened up and turned just in time to see an extremely handsome man fast closing the distance between them.

Richard Swynford stopped dead in his tracks. Before him stood the most beautiful woman he had ever seen. Her dark hair, tumbled alluringly over her shoulders, framed the face of a Da Vinci madonna. Her brilliant blue eyes glowed from the light of the fire. Her diaphanous gown did little to hide the fact that her body was as beautiful as her face. He was dumbfounded. His icy eyes flashed with emerald fire and heat rushed through his body.

Neither moved. It was some moments before he could speak.

"And just who in the devil are you?" he angrily inquired. Why such anger rose in his chest, he did not understand, but he was furious.

Katherine was too shocked to answer him for a moment. Then she realized he must be Richard, for she could plainly see his strong resemblance to Giles. She drew herself up and raised her chin ever so slightly. The Marquess lifted an eyebrow at her curiously.

"I am Katherine Swynford. And just who are you?" she replied with the sweetest smile she could muster. The rancor in her voice was not lost on the marquess.

"Swynford?" he muttered.

"Since you choose not to introduce yourself, I assume you are the Marquess of Marston." She flashed him a brilliant smile that did not reach her eyes and graciously held out her hand to him.

"Madame, at your service." He swept a mocking bow.

"I am Giles's wife, your lord," she replied.

"The devil take it! Since when?"

"Since August, my lord," she answered. Giles stirred in his sleep and she turned to him, reaching out to feel his forehead.

Richard stood silently watching the outline of her very divine figure against her gown. Crossing his arms, he leaned against the bedpost of the massive bed in an insolent manner. "It is quite obvious why Giles has married you. Do you always allow your obvious charms to be so well displayed for all to see?"

Katherine turned sharply, her face aflame with embarrassment. She realized how inapprorpriately she was dressed. Why hadn't she taken the time to put on her robe, she chided herself.

"I am in attendance on my husband. You have trespassed into our chamber, unannounced. It is most unkind of you to draw attention to my dress when it is you who have entered uninvited," she said hotly. She wanted to run from his view but refused to let him intimidate her. She stood her ground in the most dignified manner she could muster.

"State of undress would be more to the point. I congratulate Giles on his choice. You well grace any man's bedchamber." He spoke in a derisive and leering manner.

"How ungentlemanly of you," she exclaimed softly, tears now starting to sting her eyes.

"And I, for one, doubt you are a lady. To marry with the intention of becoming a rich widow hardly notes a fine character," Richard said with venom.

Katherine gasped, shocked by his accusation. How could he jump to such a vile conclusion? She raised her chin again and swept past him toward the dressing room.

"It would seem, my lord, that you might have at least inquired about the condition of your own brother. Your lack of solicitude matches your unchivalrous remarks. You obviously speak from authority on lack of character," she said. She turned her back on him and softly closed the dressing-room door.

Richard stood motionless for a moment. Damn, that woman will mean nothing but trouble, he thought. He turned to Giles. "Another of your tricks, dear brother?"

Chapter 7

Katherine crossed the room with her heart pounding and her fists tightly closed at her sides. Closing her eyes, she trembled with anger. Great heavens! she thought, just what kind of situation have I landed myself in? Never, never had she been addressed in such a crude manner! Her mind grappled with the shocking exchange she had just been part of.

Just what kind of a fiend was the Marquess? No wonder Giles had chosen the military in order to escape him. Imagine that Giles could love his home so much with a man like that living here! Why had he been so anxious to return? They could have happily remained in Dover. The trip had done him harm. . . .

Still trembling with anger, she picked up her velvet robe from where it lay on a chair and slipped into it. Standing before the mirror, she caught a glimpse of her reflection. Her pale oval face and huge eyes held a wounded look.

She picked up her brush and took control of the mass of black curls, firmly plaited them into one long braid that fell down her back. Never again would she be caught in such dishabille for those leering eyes. Damn the arrogant, truculent man.

After peeking to see if the marquess had gone, Katherine returned to Giles's bedside and took the rather comfortable chair that had purposefully been set

there. She tucked up her legs and leaned back and closed
her eyes, listening to the even breathing of her husband.

Her heart ached. Not with self-pity, but foreboding.
How far she was from her warm loving home. For the
first time, she was overwhelmed by loneliness. They had
overcome so much just to get to Marston Hall. Now,
what in heaven's name was there yet to endure? She felt
helpless. Oh Giles, recover soon, she thought. I do not
know how I shall abide your odious brother.

When Norton entered the room early in the morning,
he was delighted to see Miss Kate sleeping in the large
upholstered chair. Stirring, she opened her eyes. At the
sight of her servant, Katherine felt a rush of relief.

Here was a friend who would stand her champion.
Suddenly the ominous marquess and his vulgar manners
seemed less threatening. She could withstand his rude
remarks. She would just keep a distance between them.

"Good morning, missy. Did you manage to sleep a
little?" Norton asked as he crossed the room carrying a
large pan of warm water.

"Yes, I did," she replied, stretching her cramped
body. She rose and went to the bed to feel Giles's brow.

Giles opened his eyes. "I've made it another night,
angel. I begin to suspect you will have me around to
plague you for some time," he teased.

"So I've told you all along. And perhaps you'll find
the trial of being married to me more harrowing than
Waterloo," she teased with a lilting laugh. "Or at least,
so thinks your most charming brother."

"Richard? Is my estimable brother in residence? Has
he deigned to visit us? My, my. Have you met him?
What was his reaction to you?"

"Not favorable, I assure you! But let us not cast a
pall on this lovely day. It is time to bathe you and
change those bandages. They should have been changed
last evening, but you were far too fatigued. So behave

yourself and Norton and I will attend you," she said firmly. "We will find a physician as soon as possible."

Norton and Katherine set to work with precision and soon had Giles stripped and bathed. Katherine removed the bandages on his chest, and saw that the wound was not healing well. She knew it was because of the long journey and the jostling of the carriage. Feeling for any pronounced heat, she thought she detected an increased warmth. Katherine sighed. She bathed the area and was placing an ointment on the wound when the door opened and someone entered the room. Without looking up from her task, Katherine could tell that it was Richard. Calmly, she continued with her work.

"Good morning, Richard. Have you no greeting of welcome for me?" Giles asked.

"Indeed, welcome home, Giles. I had the pleasure of meeting your bride last night. You surprise me," he drawled in what Katherine took for an insolent manner.

Continuing to dress the wound with Norton's assistance, she deliberately chose not to acknowledge Lord Marston's presence. "Giles, shift to the left. Carefully now, while I slip this under you." She smiled in encouragement, for she knew this necessary movement was painful. Norton leaned over and helped Giles move.

Any color that might have been in his face drained as he responded to their request. He grimaced at the excruciating pain.

"I'm sorry, Giles. We're almost finished." She dropped a kiss on his forehead.

Giles smiled weakly. "My angel of mercy," he sighed.

Silently observing this interplay, Richard frowned.

Katherine continued to ignore the marquess while Norton and she slipped a fresh linen nightdress on Giles. "That should do it, until we can get a doctor in attendance, Norton. See if some broth and tea can be brought up. It is early, I know, but perhaps the cook is up and about and will accommodate us. He is far too weak,'' she sighed, and a worried frown crossed her lovely face.

"I'm sure that can be easily arranged," Richard said.

"Then see to it," she replied curtly without once glancing in his direction.

A small derisive smile appeared on Lord Marston's handsome face and he gave a slight bow in mock humility. Katherine took no notice. Lord Marston was annoyed. This beauty is a shrew, he thought. Suddenly, the idea seemed to amuse him and his cool eyes glittered.

Norton and Katherine gathered up the soiled bandages and linens. As she moved to leave the bedside, she found Lord Marston in her way. He made no move to step aside.

"Norton, I shall leave you in attendance. Thank you once more for your assistance." She beamed with great affection at Norton and turned to step around Lord Marston. Norton nodded and left to see about the broth his mistress had requested.

Richard saw the beautiful smile Katherine had given Norton fade immediately as she met his own eyes. A flash of cold ice glinted from her blue eyes as she passed by him. Giving her a nod that went totally unacknowledged, he watched her slim figure cross the room and disappear into the hall. He noted the plaited hair and remembered how it had hung free, flowing over her creamy shoulders the previous night. He stood a moment, staring at the empty door through which she had just passed. Turning sharply, he found Giles watching him with keen interest.

Richard returned the speculative look. Giles's eyes glittered with a conspiratorial gleam as he smiled with a knowing expression.

"So you have married? Why?" Richard asked.

"She's a beauty, wouldn't you say?" Giles countered.

"Aye, that she is. A rather hasty marriage, Giles. One can only wonder at your purpose."

"How can you say that, dear brother? Do you not find the state of matrimony to your satisfaction?" Giles asked with a diabolical sneer.

Richard stood silent. He paused, torn between compassion for his critically wounded brother, and the anger that caused a deep schism between them. Should he tell Giles that Lucinda was dead? He waited a moment longer.

"Perhaps, Giles, you have overreached your own duplicity this time. I have just returned last evening from Dunston. I had to carry Lucinda's body back there at the request of the Rawlings. Giles, Lucinda is dead." He looked his younger brother straight in the eyes. "So you see, you have betrayed us both."

A convulsive spasm contorted Giles's face and he cried out, "How is this? When? It was you who killed her!"

"You may look to yourself for that, Giles. I am glad she did not live to meet your ever-so-beautiful bride." Richard shifted his broad shoulders and turned to take his leave. "Let's see how the adventuress you call wife fares under your loving care. I have a feeling she is not as fragile as Lucinda."

When Katherine reached her room, she looked at the large comfortable bed with longing, for the narrow cot in the dressing room did not offer much comfort. She stood a moment and admired, for the first time, the beauty of the charmingly feminine room. The mahogany of the classic Chippendale furniture glowed softly, showing years of care. The walls were covered with pale peach damask, and from windows hung

curtains of a beautiful chintz of creamy peach and blue.
The high-posted bed was dressed in the same chintz
print and the bed cover was done in the soft damask.
The total effect was warm and welcoming.

She wondered if she would ever feel welcome in this
home. She walked over to the wardrobe and found her
clothes neatly hung inside. She chose a rose dress and
removed it from the closet.

A soft tap at the door caught her attention, and she
moved to open the door. A young girl with the rosy,
rounded look of the healthy country miss, entered the
room.

"Good morning, mistress, I am Megan, and his lordship has assigned me to be your maid. If that pleases
you, of course." Megan smiled shyly and dropped a
curtsy.

"Certainly, Megan. That is most kind." Katherine
smiled sweetly for she could see the girl was somewhat
nervous.

Megan's blue eyes twinkled over her freckled nose
and cheeks. She was delighted by the warm reception of
her new mistress. No high-toned city lady here, she
thought with a great deal of relief.

"Mrs. Swynford, this is my first assignment as a
ladies' maid so do let me know how to go on. I aim to
please ye, I do," she said.

Katherine laughed. "Then we both shall learn, for I
am the daughter of a doctor and have never had a
ladies' maid."

Megan grinned broadly in delight at her good
fortune.

Two footmen knocked at the door and carried in a
hip-bathtub and several maids followed with buckets of
hot steaming water. After quickly preparing the bath,
they bowed in respect and left. Katherine was surprised,
but pleased. A bath would be heavenly, she thought.

Megan bustled about, pouring scented oil in the water and laying large towels out upon a chair. She placed a screen in front of the tub. As she assisted Katherine out of her robe and nightdress, she thought young Giles had indeed chosen a beautiful wife.

Katherine was a little uncomfortable with such attention, but slipped gratefully into the warm scented water. She closed her eyes a moment and let the sensual warmth of the water caress her skin and relax her tired muscles.

Later, Megan toweled her dry until her skin glowed. She helped Katherine into her clothes, tying ribbons and buttoning tiny buttons. Katherine couldn't help but smile at such ministrations and Megan smiled back in appreciation. She then brushed Katherine's hair and twisted it up on her head, artfully arranging stray tendrils along Katherine's cheeks and weaving a rose ribbon through her rich dark curls.

"There, ye are fit to meet the Regent himself!" She laughed.

"Megan, I'm sure you're quite right."

"Lady Amelia has asked me to show you to the breakfast room. She awaits ye there, most anxious to make your acquaintance." Megan curtsied again and moved to open the door.

Katherine picked up a fine Norwich shawl which had been a gift from her father and began to follow Megan through the long corridors. She stared in fascination at the ancient armor that hung on the walls, but was even more interested in Megan's words. She turned her attention on the young maid.

"Lady Amelia? I am afraid I do not know all the members of this household," Katherine said.

Megan glanced at her in surprise. "She is Master Giles's aunt—sister to his departed father. A kind lady, you'll find."

"Who are the other members of the family, Megan?" Katherine asked as she followed the young maid through the long halls.

" 'Tis sad, but his lordship is recently widowed. Lady Marston died last week, leaving the wee Ellen without a mother," Megan said. A frown furrowed her young brow as she pursed her mouth in disapproval.

Katherine stopped a moment. "You mean the marquess has just lost his wife? He has a daughter?"

"Didn't ye know?" Megan asked.

"No, Giles did not speak much of his family, and of course, he has been so critically ill . . ." she answered, and let the matter drop. Why hadn't Giles even mentioned the other members of his family? How strange, Katherine thought.

Chapter 8

Katherine entered the sunny breakfast room and found Lady Amelia sitting at the table, partaking of an enormous breakfast.

The older woman looked up and smiled in genuine greeting.

"My dear, I am Giles's aunt Amelia, and I'm so pleased to meet you." She fluttered her hands as she spoke. She was a small woman, dressed in a black bombazine mourning dress. Her keen brown eyes studied Katherine from under a crown of snow-white hair.

"Thank you, Lady Amelia. I am also pleased to make your acquaintance," Katherine returned her smile as she took a seat at the table.

Lady Amelia immediately noted the confidence this very young lady seemed to command. She raised an eyebrow in wonder. She would not have thought Giles would choose so self-possessed a young woman. Her curiosity was instantly aroused.

"Do have something to eat, my dear," she said, nodding to a footman standing by to assist Katherine.

The young man took up a plate and awaited Katherine's choice from the many dishes on the sideboard.

Katherine sat a moment, not quite understanding the procedure.

"Do try some of the kippers, they are delicious. I also

recommend the kidneys and ham," Amelia encouraged her, fluttering delicately again.

"My, such choices. I should soon grow quite fat. Some ham and toast, please," Katherine said.

The footman quickly filled the plate and placed it in front of her.

"Add a divine sweet roll, James," Lady Amelia said, winking at Katherine. "They are exceptionally good."

Katherine was delighted with this sprightly lady. She was like a breath of fresh air after her meetings with the lord of the manor. Relaxing under this lady's kind manner, Katherine picked up her fork to begin her meal.

"Katherine, we are consumed with curiosity. How did you meet Giles? It all sounds so romantic, for we did not know he was even interested in a young lady." Lady Amelia nodded to the servant to be excused. Servants, she thought, learned soon enough about everything that went on in a household.

When the question was put to her, Katherine was suddenly at a loss to explain her marriage to Giles. It had seemed so right at the time, but now it had begun to seem rather unusual even to herself. She was wife in name only. Though a deep friendship had grown between them on the journey home, it was as if Giles wanted nothing more than that. Of course, he was desperately ill and could not play the lover. Still, it was strange how he treated her—sometimes flirtatious, but never showing any signs of deeper emotion. All along Katherine had attributed her husband's lack of ardor to his grave condition. Yet she had found no deeper attachment growing within her own heart and lately this had begun to worry her.

Her father had, perhaps, been correct. She had married too hastily and for the wrong reasons. But how could she tell an elderly family member she did not know, what she did not understand herself? The question forcibly brought into focus the nagging thoughts she had pushed back and refused to examine.

"I met Giles in Dover, where my father is a physician. We became friends before he was sent to the Continent. When he returned, so terribly wounded, my father took him in and saved his life. His wounds are very serious. He should have remained in Dover, but could think of nothing but returning to Marston Hall. It became an obsession," Katherine said, intentionally skirting any emotional aspects.

"Marston Hall has always been an obsession with Giles," Lady Amelia answered dryly. Then as if to cover her words, she smiled vaguely and added, "But then who wouldn't feel thus? You shall be equally enchanted too, I'm sure. So he fell in love with you, and brought you home. How charming a story," she said again with the same helpless flutter of her many-ringed fingers.

Watching her, Katherine suddenly felt the lady's eyes did not agree with the words that came from her mouth. Katherine did not reply but began to eat the food set before her.

Richard Swynford entered the room with his usual firm step and purposefulness. Katherine had to admit he looked striking in a blue riding coat that fit his broad shoulders to perfection and buckskin pantaloons that displayed his muscled legs. He moved with confident, athletic grace, and his strong, handsome features were set in a noncommittal expression as he passed her. He smiled at his aunt and placed a hand on her shoulder as he walked by her.

"Good morning, Aunt Amelia. I see you have met Giles's bride," he said, his low, resonant voice archly emphasizing the word *bride*. He gave Katherine a curt nod.

She noted the black band he wore on his arm and wondered if he had worn one the previous evening. She had not noticed one before now, but she had been vastly upset by his behavior so it could have easily slipped her observation.

She gave him a small tentative smile and continued eating.

As if they had stood ready for his entrance, two servants promptly entered the room to attend Lord Marston. They certainly respond to his lordship, Katherine thought derisively. He must be quite a task-master, just as Giles suggested.

"I must be excused, for I should return to Giles now," Katherine said, rising from her chair and turning an icy smile on the marquess. "Have you sent for the doctor, my lord? It is imperative that you do so." Her cool, measured voice carried a decided hauteur.

"Aye, he has been sent for," Richard answered. He studied her face, his curiosity about this young woman aroused.

Katherine nodded and gracefully swept from the room, carrying herself with all the dignity she could muster.

"Well, she certainly is a beauty," Amelia commented.

"One could not fault that observation, Amelia," Richard answered with a decided frown.

Amelia cast her nephew a questioning look. Ignoring it, Richard turned his attention to the food placed before him.

Katherine took her place next to Giles's bedside. He was awake but pale and listless.

"How do you feel, Giles?" she asked as she rose to feel his brow. It was warm.

"Don't plague me with your damn questions! How do you expect me to feel?" he replied, closing his eyes.

Aghast, Katherine turned to look at Norton. Norton shrugged his broad shoulders.

"He's been out of sorts this morning, missy," Norton began to explain.

"Just leave me be!" Giles interjected.

Katherine nodded to Norton and he quietly left the room. She sat once more in the chair, saying nothing. She was silent for some time.

Giles opened his eyes. "Ah, faithful Kate, still here. Are you always so devoted?" he mocked.

Katherine's eyes grew large with surprise. "It would seem so, Giles. Do not fret, I know it is just a bad day for you," she coaxed.

"Little you know of it . . ."

Just then, the marquess entered the room with a short, rotund gentleman.

"Dr. Carleton is here to examine Giles. May I present Mrs. Swynford to you," he said curtly.

"Doctor, I fear he has had a setback. He seems to be somewhat feverish." Katherine's words tumbled out in a rush.

"Madame, I appreciate your concern, but if you do not mind, I will determine the condition of the patient," Dr. Carleton replied haughtily.

Katherine narrowed her eyes. The florid-faced, arrogant doctor was so unlike her kind, capable father, she thought.

"Excuse us please, while I examine the patient," he continued.

Katherine stood to watch the procedure and offer assistance.

"Madame, please leave. I shall inform you of my findings," the doctor snapped.

Stunned, Katherine turned in appeal to Lord Marston, her beautiful eyes full of concern.

Richard merely nodded his assent. A pang stabbed his heart at her stricken face.

"Very well, I shall await your findings in the hall, doctor," Katherine said in a voice barely above a whisper. She cast Richard a scathing look as she turned to go.

"Mrs. Swynford, wait in my library. We will join you there," Richard called to her as she left the room.

After asking directions, she found her way to the library, which was a masculine room with rich mahogany paneling and beautiful Turkish rugs. As she walked over to the library stacks and began to peruse the vast collection her anger began to fade.

Katherine was thrilled when she came across a small ancient Book of Hours. She took the beautiful illuminated manuscript to the large window to examine it. She lovingly fingered the delicate artwork that had been created by a monk some several centuries past.

Katherine became so engrossed in the book that it seemed only a short time later that Dr. Carleton was escorted by the marquess into the library. Anticipation and apprehension showed on her comely face as she waited for him to speak.

A patronizing expression was pasted upon the pretentious doctor's florid face. He addressed Katherine in a tone that seemed to indicate she was either a child or the village idiot. She pursed her mouth and narrowed her eyes.

"Madame, I must inform you that your husband is critically ill," he said as he feigned what he felt was appropriate concern.

Katherine raised one eyebrow in utter disgust. "Your medical observation amazes me. I find your statement an utter surprise," she sarcastically replied.

Dr. Carleton flushed, as he had the grace to feel some discomfiture at his totally inane statement. The marquess observed this exchange with as much surprise as the egotistical doctor.

"I am the daughter of a very competent physician and

have assisted him for several years. What treatment do you propose?'' she asked, her disgust still obvious.

"Ahem, rest, of course, and I have left a sedative so that he might rest . . .'' Dr. Carleton mumbled.

"But the infection that seems to be mounting?'' she asked. "Hot poultices, perhaps?'' she continued. "Should not the wound be opened and cleansed before it turns to gangrene?''

Dr. Carleton stood flabbergasted at her impertinence. "I should like to watch Captain Swynford for a day or two before I make that judgement. It is a dangerous operation,'' he replied. "It is best to wait and see,'' he continued, running his fat fingers along his collar.

"Then it shall be too late,'' Katherine said emphatically. She turned to Richard Swynford. "The man is incompetent.''

Richard blinked at her in amazement. The chit seemed to know what she was talking about. Her audacity and confidence intrigued him, for he had never encountered a woman who spoke with such authority.

"Thank you, Dr. Carleton, for answering our call to you so promptly. Now I shall have to show you out,'' the marquess said as he began to usher the portly man from the room.

Katherine placed the book upon the desk and walked around it to meet the marquess when he turned toward her. Her fists were tightly closed, her cheeks red, and her eyes glinting. She was ready for a fight. She moved to within inches of him and raised her face to his.

Richard looked down on her with a surprisingly kind expression. "Do you know of what you speak?'' he asked.

"Indeed, I do not have the knowledge to perform the operation myself but I know more than that pompous—'' She stopped short of the word she wished to use.

A small smile lifted the corners of Richard's mouth.

He could have filled in that word, he thought in amusement. "I shall find the man who can do the job as soon as possible," he reassured her.

"Thank you. But make all haste; I fear for Giles. He has suddenly changed his attitude. He seems so listless."

Richard looked into her lovely, worried eyes and wondered at her seemingly genuine concern. Giles had obviously made a conquest of this beautiful woman. But then, he had always been adept at stealing women's hearts.

"I shall attend this matter as soon as possible." He bowed and turned to leave the room. "You may feel free to avail yourself of this library anytime you wish."

Katherine did not have time to reply before he was gone. He had surprised her by accepting her opinion.

Chapter 9

Richard Swynford left the room to find his secretary, Mr. Palmer, to give him instructions to go to New Castle upon Tyne in order to secure the services of Dr. Deane. The doctor was reputed to be excellent, but it would be two days before Mr. Palmer could bring the physician to Marston. To Richard's surprise, he found himself concerned that those two days might prove to be too long a wait for Giles.

After giving the instructions to the thin, bespectacled Mr. Palmer, Richard changed into riding breeches and coat. He needed to escape the manor with all its swirling emotions. A long hard ride over his estates was the exercise he needed, he thought.

His spurs softly clinked as he crossed the lower hall. As he passed the long gallery, he observed Katherine standing in front of the large portrait of Lucinda. He frowned. I must have that painting removed, he thought. A hand as cold as ice gripped his heart.

He started to direct his footsteps down the hall that would lead him to the courtyard but instead found himself walking toward Katherine. Her presence was beginning to haunt him. He did not doubt for a minute that she was a mere adventuress who had seized a golden opportunity. A physician's daughter married into the house of Swynford was an opportunist's dream come true. It was amazing, he thought, how women of great beauty often possessed the most calculating natures.

Katherine turned at the sound of spurs on the parquet floor. She watched the marquess coming toward her and her heart leaped at his fierce expression. Her eyes widened and held his unwavering gaze.

He stopped very close to her. Slowly, he tore his gaze from hers and let his eyes travel to the portrait. His delicate blond wife stared down at him with a pensive, detached expression. Richard recognized the weakness in her beautiful face. For the first time, he suspected her life with him must have been her own private hell. He knew he should never have married her. Still, he had been charmed by her fragile, helpless air—so different from that of the young woman who stood next to him, he thought. This one, he thought, seizes life for herself.

Katherine was electrifyingly aware of the marquess's nearness. Her breathing shortened as his arm brushed her shoulder and she felt totally disconcerted.

"She was very beautiful, my lord," she managed to say. "I offer my condolences. It must be a dreadful loss for you." Katherine turned to look at Richard.

A closed look came into his eyes and his face hardened in a mask. "Yes, well, I'm sure she will be missed," he said in a cold, detached voice. He gave a slight bow, then turned on his heel and quickly walked away.

What a cold, strange man, Katherine thought as she watched him go. Either he carries no grief, or he is a master at hiding his emotions. How could two brothers be so different, she wondered.

Quickly putting the marquess from her mind, she made her way upstairs to Giles's bedroom. She found him resting. His pallor was more pronounced. She took her chair next to him, as Norton left the room.

"Giles, how do you feel? Can I get anything you

might want? Do you wish me to read to you?" she inquired.

"Kate, just sit there. I just need you there, that is all. Faithful Kate. I have done you an injustice . . ." His voice faded as he drifted out of consciousness.

Poor, dear Giles, she thought. This is so hard for him. Pray God he improves soon. I do not think he will fare well if he does not soon show some improvement. She shook her head sadly.

Lady Amelia softly entered the room followed by Maddy, her maid, who was carrying Katherine's warm wool cape.

"My dear, I shall sit awhile with Giles. You need some fresh air before luncheon. It is not healthy for you to sit here all the time. Giles is sleeping. He will not miss you. If he does need you, I shall summon you immediately," she said with gentle concern.

Katherine rose and gave Lady Amelia a smile of gratitude. "Thank you, Aunt Amelia. You are correct. I shall surely enjoy that ever so much!"

"Katherine, Nanny Burke has little Ellen in the small walled garden. Richard's daughter will enchant you. Children have a way of lightening our burdens. Don't you agree? Why don't you join them in their outing?" Lady Amelia said as she picked up a book and sat down beside the patient.

Maddy escorted Katherine to the entrance of the small garden. Tucking her cloak around her, Katherine stepped into the charming little courtyard. High stone walls protected against any chilling breeze, and autumn flowers still lingered in their beds. The merry laughter of a child drifted to her on the air.

Katherine crossed the small stone walk and took a seat on the stone bench, next to a matronly nurse and the little girl.

"I am Katherine Swynford."

"Aye, and I am called Nanny Burke. This is young Ellen," said the rotund, rosy woman holding Ellen. She was a short woman with great kind eyes that twinkled with good humor.

Ellen laid her head shyly on her nanny's shoulder and watched the new lady with interest. She was delicately built with fair hair, golden-brown eyes, and two enchanting dimples that appeared when she smiled.

"I am delighted to meet you, Ellen," Katherine said as she reached out to touch her hand. Ellen drew back and buried her face in Nanny Burke's neck.

"She's a bit shy, my lady. But she'll come around, for she is as affectionate a babe as ye'll ever find," Nanny said with a chuckle as she jostled her charge. Ellen laughed. She peeked up at Katherine, her light brown eyes sparkling with interest.

Katherine fell into a light banter with Nanny and directed many remarks to Ellen. It wasn't too long before Ellen was clinging to Katherine's hand as they knelt to pat a kitten that had crawled out from under the stone bench.

"Such a pretty kitten. What is his name?" Kate asked.

"Meow, 'cause that's what he says," Ellen importantly informed her.

"Meow, what a perfect name. I like it," she said, rising from her crouched position. She ruffled the child's golden hair.

She was delighted with the little girl and vowed to spend some time each day with her. Katherine was concerned, for she knew the child had just lost her mother, and it would do them both good to have some light-hearted play.

"Nanny Burke, please allow me to join you again. She is a dear. It is good to laugh . . ." Katherine's voice faded and her eyes clouded. Thinking of the child's severe father, she felt sure Ellen needed more attention.

"Aye, that it is. You'll be doing wee Ellen a kindness too. She needs a woman's attention," the nurse said.

Katherine flashed her an understanding look, but did not know that Nanny Burke was referring to the fact that the child's mother had often been too occupied to spend much time with her.

Katherine took Ellen to the kitchen where they armed themselves with leftover bread. They walked hand in hand outside to the small man-made pond at the lower end of the sloping back terrace. There, they happily cast crumbs to the ducks and swans that gathered, loudly squawking around them. Ellen laughed at the antics of the tame waterfowl. She squealed with delight when one rather bold fellow came right up to them in order to retrieve a morsel. Sitting together, they fed the ducks and swans until it was time for luncheon.

Lady Amelia and Katherine ate luncheon together, for Lord Marston had not returned from his ride over his estates. Katherine then returned to her post as Giles's beside.

She slipped away for a little rest before it was time to dress for dinner. Pausing at the door of the wardrobe in which her clothes had been neatly hung, she silently debated about what would be proper to wear. The household was in mourning, of course, but was it proper for her to wear mourning for a woman she had never met? She wished she had spoken to Lady Amelia about it at luncheon, but it had not occurred to her until now. There were so many concerns and events running through her very tired mind that until this instant she had not even considered it. She sighed, for it all seemed so confusing. Though Lady Amelia certainly had been most kind, Katherine still felt like an outsider in her new family. Well, she thought, she would just have to make the best of it all. She prayed that Giles would recover swiftly and hoped she would be able to tolerate his odious brother.

She decided on a modest silk lavender gown trimmed in dark blue ribbons. It would have to do, for she had no black dresses in her possession. Since lavender was often used for half mourning, it would be the most appropriate choice. I shall have to speak to Lady Amelia about what is proper for me, she mused.

Megan insisted on helping her dress. To Katherine it still seemed so silly for a grown woman to need help donning a dress. Of course, the attention was nice and buttons down the back of a gown were impossible to fasten alone. Megan also was proving positively remarkable in arranging her hair.

When she was at last ready, she took a long, appraising look at herself. The toll that the long journey and difficult events of Giles's illness had taken showed in the dark circles under her eyes. She was tired, but perhaps that night she would rest better. She sighed and shrugged her shoulders. What did it matter anyway? She was not intent on impressing anyone, certainly not the arrogant marquess.

Lord Marston and Lady Amelia were deep in conversation when Katherine entered the salon. She paused a moment, again feeling like an interloper. Richard turned his uncomfortably penetrating hazel-green eyes to her.

"Come in, my dear. Join us for a bit of sherry before dinner." Lady Amelia beckoned in genuine welcome.

Katherine accepted the wine proffered her by Richard with a tentative smile and seated herself on a fine Chippendale settee. She sat regally, emanating assurance she did not feel.

Richard studied her for a moment, then glanced toward Lady Amelia. His aunt returned his gaze with a great deal of interest. Richard turned his attention immediately to Katherine, asking, "How goes it with Giles this evening?"

"He is resting well, my lord. However, he does need

the attention of the physician. I fear time is of the utmost importance. I worry—'' She dropped her eyes to the glass of golden sherry.

"It is my belief that he should be here no later than the day after tomorrow. We can only hope that will be soon enough," Richard replied with resignation.

Katherine's eyes flew to his, flashing with anger. "I'm afraid I cannot match your complacent attitude, sir!"

Lady Amelia uttered a small gasp and was infinitely relieved when Latimer announced dinner was served.

Richard took his aunt's arm and turned to extend his hand to Katherine, but she strolled past him as if she had not noticed. Lady Amelia's eyes gleamed with amusement, and she mustered all her tact to allow only a barest hint of a smile.

Dinner actually proved to be pleasant. Lady Amelia extended herself with her fluttering chatter. Richard, who acknowledged the appropriateness of Katherine's setdown, joined in the conversation, making every effort to appear the perfect host. Katherine's natural buoyancy and good humor showed in her response to their efforts.

"Richard, as soon as Katherine feels she can take a bit of time away from Giles, you must take her to see Merrywood. It is to be her home and I'm sure Giles will want to move there as soon as he is able. Perhaps she might want to make changes. I'm sure it needs work on the interiors, with Giles gone so long. Don't you agree?'' Amelia added just as they were to leave the table.

"Indeed. Katherine, allow me to show you Merrywood. It is a lovely manor house. I'm sure you shall like it. Shall we consider the excursion after Dr. Deane has seen Giles? We'll know a bit more how to go on when we hear his opinion," he said with an intense expression in his eyes.

Katherine's heart skipped a beat. He seemed to overwhelm her when he looked at her that way. She could not understand it. She was not intimidated by him, but it sometimes seemed that he filled all the space between them.

"I should like to see my future home very much. Thank you for the invitation, but we must first see how Giles fares before I can turn my attention to the needs of Merrywood." She smiled and the sapphire light of her eyes lit her whole face.

My, she is beautiful beyond comparison, Richard thought. He closed off that train of thought immediately. "Let us retire to the salon. I shall not take port alone tonight but will join you," he stated as he rose and placed his napkin on the table.

"Thank you again, but I am most fatigued. May I be excused to retire to my room?" Katherine asked as she too rose to take her leave.

"Indeed, my dear, you must be totally drained of energy. Do sleep well," Lady Amelia said kindly.

"Lady Amelia, I have meant to ask about the household being in mourning. I have no mourning clothes. Is it not proper for me to go into mourning in respect for both of you and your loss?"

"It is not necessary. You did not even know Lucinda," Richard answered stiffly. "However, it might be advisable to purchase some mourning dresses, if all does not go well with Giles."

A silence fell over the room. Time seemed to be frozen in space at Richard's tactless observation.

"Richard!" exclaimed Lady Amelia as she turned a shocked face to her nephew. "How utterly thoughtless!"

"I shall take the thought under advisement, my lord," Katherine answered quietly as she left the room.

She crossed the hall and was about to mount the staircase. She heard the hurrying footsteps in pursuit and turned to see Richard. He reached out and took her arm.

"Forgive me, Katherine, that is twice tonight I have spoken without regard to your feelings. Amelia says I am a barbarian to have spoken so thoughtlessly. I beg your pardon. It is a fault of mine to be too forthright, and I vow not to be so again."

"It is forgotten, my lord. It matters not." She gave him a nod and moved up the stairs.

He stood a moment, watching her retreating figure. Damn, he thought. He withdrew to his study for a brandy.

Chapter 10

Richard removed his neckcloth and tossed it aside in irritation. He had long since shed his jacket and boots and now stood looking out of his bedroom window onto the moonlit garden. His left hand held back the drape as his right hand unbuttoned his shirt in a slow deliberate manner.

The brandy he had consumed by the fire had not dulled the memory of those blue eyes staring at him first in disbelief, then disdain. No matter how hard he tried to forget, the image still lingered. Why does it bother me so much, he wondered. No answer was forthcoming. He stood a moment longer, then turned swiftly, letting the drape drop as he crossed the room to the huge four-poster bed draped in russet damask.

He stretched his long frame out on the bed and put his hands behind his head. He made no move to remove his clothes and prepare for sleep. Thank heavens he had dismissed Robbins, he mused, for he could not stand his ministrations tonight, however discreet they might be. Robbins always seemed to anticipate his master's moods and adapted to them perfectly.

Tonight no one could suit his mood, unless . . . Richard's vision of Katherine standing at the bottom of the staircase suddenly changed to the one he had seen when he first laid eyes on her. Remembering how her flowing hair tumbled down around her shoulders and how the firelight revealed her feminine curves, he felt a stirring of desire spread like fire through his body.

He closed his eyes as if to shut out her memory. Why does she haunt me so tonight, he wondered. He shifted on the bed to make himself more comfortable. But it was his thoughts, not the bed, that made him uncomfortable.

She is just a common adventuress, he told himself. One well versed in how to manipulate men with those large innocent-looking blue eyes. So, he reasoned, she excited him sexually. Many women could do that. He would dismiss the whole idea of her. Let the unfortunate Giles deal with her. She'll run him a merry chase, he thought as if to comfort himself with the idea.

There was a hidden passion in her that intrigued him. A passion that had not yet been awakened. Richard dismissed that thought, reasoning that surely Giles had claimed his conjugal rights. Still, Giles had married her after he was wounded and no man as injured and ill as he was could make love to a woman. That thought filled Richard with pleasure and dismay.

Why in the devil's name would he care if Giles had bedded her? He hadn't cared one iota after the initial shock and anger of discovering Giles had seduced Lucinda. Lucinda, he thought, poor vapid Lucinda. Remembering the pale fragile beauty who had once seemed so lightly charming, he wondered why he had married her. In the beginning her helplessness had made him feel strong and protective. He had been twenty-six at the time and knew he should settle down with a wife and raise a family. Lucinda had seemed the perfect candidate. She had beauty, excellent family connections, and always managed to be agreeable. It was as if she had not lived in the real world.

For the first time the thought occurred to him that perhaps the Rawlins family had sought the marriage more than Lucinda. For she had been no more prepared to be his wife than could possibly be imagined. She had rejected him.

He remembered all too well the terrible scene on their wedding night. He had expected a shy bride who would need gentle wooing, not the shocked, screaming shrew whose voice had carried through the halls for all to hear.

How clearly he could remember that night. When he had entered her chamber, Lucinda had looked like a pale angel in shimmering white lace. She had stood smiling in welcome as he approached her and took her into his arms. He had kissed her gently first. But when he had lifted her to the bed and begun to remove her gown, he could feel her stiffen. When his mouth trailed down her neck to her breast, she began to struggle and pushed him away.

With tears streaming down her cheeks she cried hysterically at what he was doing. He had made the error of then removing his dressing gown, at which point Lucinda broke free, scrambling from the bed.

"Don't touch me! You brute, don't ever touch me! You're disgusting!" she cried. "Leave me, leave me, I hate you! You're disgusting."

Richard froze, foolishly holding his robe, momentarily speechless. "Lucinda, didn't anyone tell you what was expected in a marriage?" he finally managed.

"Yes, no, I mean . . . it's disgusting! Just leave me be!" She cried uncontrollably, her whole body racked with sobs as she huddled on the floor.

Richard been been aghast. He remembered turning to the door as growing anger began to consume him. He walked out of the door to the sound of her pitiful sobs and had never entered it again.

Richard shifted on his bed. The anger had long been gone, but the memory remained vivid. How had Giles

gotten to her, he wondered. He had used his light charm
with calculated perfidy. He had taken time, patience,
and flattery. Flowery words! Richard frowned.

He knew he himself had not cared enough to woo her.
He had wondered ever since why he even had married
her. God, her life must have been hell. Richard's
conscience pricked him for he had virtually ignored her
after that first night. He knew he had been barely civil
to her. No wonder Giles had been able to win her. In the
darkest part of his heart he had been glad, for he had
reached the point where he could no longer abide her
and her simpering ways, and she had known it.

Richard sat up and buried his face in his hands. Was
he responsible for Lucinda's death? No, he knew that
was not true. She had taken her own life in her misery
over Giles. Though it was he who had banished Giles—
it was Lucinda who had chosen to tie her horse and
wade into the river. Most said she had fallen in the water
by accident, but Richard knew otherwise. The horse had
been tied to the tree.

"Enough," he said out loud, as if to banish the
haunting memories. He eased his weary body off the
bed. He removed his clothes, letting them drop to the
floor, and slipped under the covers. He willed himself to
think of estate and agricultural matters, defying his
morose memories to return. Yet, just before he finally
drifted off to sleep, the image of a pair of blue eyes
flashed once more through his consciousness.

Katherine had left Richard standing at the bottom of
the steps. She had accepted his apology, grudgingly, she
admitted. He was so blunt—the antithesis of glib, light-
hearted Giles. If it weren't for their marked physical
resemblance, one would have never guessed they were
brothers. Giles was all charm while Richard seemed
determined to be annoyingly candid. Her mind

pondered the differences between brothers as she made her way to see Giles.

She entered the sickroom to find the ever-faithful Norton keeping watch. She glanced at Giles, who was sleeping, and then to Norton. "How is he this evening? He was so restless this afternoon. I am concerned. The doctor must get here soon," she whispered, hoping not to disturb her husband.

Norton shrugged his shoulders and shook his head. "Miss Kate, he has just now gone to sleep. He has been delirious most of the evening. I did not call you, for there was naught you could do. We can only wait for the doctor. I've tried to bathe his forehead but he only pushes me away."

"Dear Norton, how I appreciate all you have done for me. I shall get ready for bed and then relieve you until later. You must now rest yourself." She smiled fondly at the hulking man who had for so long watched over her.

Katherine left for her own chambers and readied herself for bed. She plaited her long hair and donned a heavy velvet robe, for the autumn evenings were now turning quite chilly. She returned to Giles's chamber and bid Norton a good evening.

"Call me missy if ye need me. I'll come before dawn to relieve you," Norton reminded her before he left.

Katherine soaked a cloth in cool water from the pitcher on the washstand and bathed Giles's face and neck. He barely stirred beneath her ministrations and her heart sank with foreboding. If the doctor didn't arrive the next day, they would surely lose him.

Katherine wearily sank down on the chair. She sat quietly for a moment, her hands idly toying with the ribbon belt of her robe. The room was completely still except for the shadows cast by the fire in the grate and the soft ticking of a clock on the mantelpiece.

Giles stirred and a soft moan escaped his lips. With each tick of the clock his breathing seemed to become more labored. Suddenly the possibility of his death became a firm reality. She had always understood how gravely ill he was, but until then she had faith he would recover, just as he had overcome the odds of that dangerous journey.

She should have listened to her father and refused to bring him home until he had fully recovered. He could not have made the journey without Norton and her to care for him. They should have simply refused. My dear Lord, she prayed silently, have I done so wrong? Why had she listened to his pleas? Katherine wept.

Katherine slowly raised her head from her hands, her cheeks wet with tears. Richard was right! He knew! He had warned her to buy mourning clothes because he knew! However blunt he was, he was right. Still, she wondered how he could speak of the possible death of his own brother with such callous detachment. How cold he was. Why had Giles wanted so desperately to come to this hateful place? Surely they could have been happy in Dover. What motive had driven Giles to return to Marston Hall when so much animosity seemed to exist between him and his brother?

She couldn't understand such a family, for the one she had grown up in was so loving. How could people be so uncaring? Angrily, she thought of the lack of interest Lord Marston showed in his own daughter.

The image of Richard's dark, handsome features came into her mind. There was something hidden within him. He had genuinely seemed to regret his tactlessness when he had apologized. She had seen a look of concern deep in his eyes that almost could have been tenderness. No, she would not believe that it could have been. But he had regretted his unkind remark. Was there more to Richard Swynford than she had given him credit for?

Deep within her heart she knew there was, for she had glimpsed the hurt behind the arrogance in those icy eyes.

Once more a sense of loneliness overwhelmed her. Perhaps Giles would survive. She'd see to it. He must!

Chapter 11

The sound of clattering hooves and rattling wheels in the courtyard announced that the long-awaited Dr. Deane had arrived. Latimer sent servants scurrying to inform the marquess and rushed outside to assist the travelers.

Richard had just returned from his morning tour of the estate and was still wearing his buckskin riding clothes. He was with the bailiff when the young footman, Jepson, rushed in to inform him of the doctor's arrival.

"Your lordship, Latimer wishes you to know that Dr. Deane has arrived with Mr. Palmer. They are now in the courtyard. Is there anything you wish me to do?"

Richard nodded. "Has Mrs. Swynford been informed? If not, see that she is," he directed, and turned his attention to the bailiff, Mr. Cooper. "You can take care of this matter, I am sure. Summon me if you need me otherwise, I shall be taken up with the needs of my brother."

"Yes, your lordship, I'll tend to all this. 'Tis simple enough a business," the bailiff anxiously assured him.

Richard quickly strode out of the estate office that was situated at the back entrance of the manor. He saw Katherine fairly flying down the staircase as he entered the front hall. Her cheeks were flushed and her eyes sparkled with anticipation.

"Thank God, they are here at last!" she cried.

He had no time to comment, for just then the doctor entered with Mr. Palmer. Little time was wasted in introductions and the common courtesies since Dr. Deane had traveled fast and hard to answer this summons.

Katherine led the way, and Dr. Deane and Richard followed. They entered Giles's bedchamber to find the patient lucid and watchful. He seemed listless but alert as Dr. Deane began his examination.

Later, Dr. Deane presented his findings to Richard and Katherine in the library. Katherine was reassured by his expert knowledge and direct approach. He gave her the same kind of confidence her father had always given her, and she could feel her body relax.

"I will tell you what you already know. He is gravely ill. The deep musket-ball wound in his chest is not healing. Mr. Palmer informed me of his journey here and I'm sure the jolting aggravated his injuries. However, the wounds are severe and I cannot say he would have healed properly in any case. I should like to open up the wound and reclean it, for I am certain it is infected and will turn gangrene unless it is treated immediately. Unfortunately, the operation will be very painful for Captain Swynford." He spoke with an authority that precluded disagreement.

"What room will afford me the best light?" he asked the marquess.

Richard paused a moment, then replied. "The breakfast room. It has full windows and allows the most light."

"Then let us have it prepared immediately," the doctor said as he turned to Katherine. "It is my understanding, you have assisted your father. Would you be capable of helping me operate on your own husband?"

Katherine's heart began to pound. She had assumed

he would request her help, but when the question was asked, she faltered. She turned toward Richard with a questioning look. His cool eyes met hers and he nodded slightly.

"Yes, yes, of course. I have had much experience and would hope to assist you." Her own voice seemed far away to her and she trembled.

Dr. Deane excused himself and at the direction of a footman was ushered to his room to prepare himself for the operation.

Katherine stood a moment after he left, then began to leave in order to change her pale silk morning dress. She felt Richard's hand on her arm and turned.

"You have been at Giles's side almost constantly. Are you too fatigued to do this? Is it too much to ask?" His voice was soft and full of kindness.

She stood looking at him a moment, feeling the warmth of his hand on her arm. She needed to be comforted, and the kindness in his voice almost caused her to collapse into his arms.

Whether or not Richard felt that momentary lapse, she did not know. She quickly stepped away from him and answered, "Have no fear. I can do it. I'm sure of it."

Richard dropped his hand and smiled. "Good, he needs you. I shall see that the preparations are being made. Norton and I will meet you in Giles's room."

Within the hour all had been prepared. Giles had been gently moved and given enough brandy to make his senses dull. A cloth had been placed in his mouth for him to bite down on when the pain became too great.

Katherine's training served her well and she assisted Dr. Deane so ably that he once looked up and winked at her. That wink spoke volumes, for he was a strict and meticulous physician.

Giles suffered the agonies of his wounds, all over

again. He cried out, but the sounds were muffled by his mouth guard. It was a mercy that when the pain became unbearably excruciating he fainted.

Sweat poured down Katherine's back and forehead. She could feel it run between her breasts as the tension mounted. Still, she was able to hand the necessary tools and cloths to Dr. Deane as he needed them.

The ordeal seemed to last forever. A wave of nausea came over Katherine and she thought she might faint. Finally, the excruciating task was finished. Norton and the marquess moved Giles onto the stretcher and two husky footmen carried him to his bedchamber.

Katherine untied her blood-soaked apron and let it fall to the floor with the other soaked cloths. Her simple cotton gown was also covered with blood but she took no notice. Slowly she climbed the stairs to follow the others, her legs feeling like heavy weights and wobbly underpins.

Lady Amelia emerged from the front salon and rushed to take Katherine's arm when she noted her extreme pallor. "My dear, allow me to assist you! How brave you are. My admiration is beyond expression. I wonder if Giles knows what a courageous wife he has. Men seldom do. Still he must, for I shall tell him!" Amelia quickly rattled on. She held Katherine's arm with care and concern as they slowly climbed the steps and made their way through the hall to Giles's bedchamber. Katherine smiled wanly and patted dear Amelia's hand.

Richard turned at their entrance and watched Katherine keenly. Noticing his eyes never left Katherine, Amelia cocked an eyebrow.

"I am well satisfied," Dr. Deane announced. "Now it is in the hands of the Almighty. I shall sit beside him for a while to be sure there's no bleeding. I have given him a sedative, enough for him to sleep several hours without stirring. That is most important." Dr. Deane drew up a chair with the same authority he had displayed since his arrival. He glanced over to Katherine.

She was leaning against the bed, her hand around the heavy carved post. She seemed barely able to stand.

"Get that young lady to bed," Dr. Deane snapped.

Richard rushed to Katherine's side. He put an arm around her waist and felt her knees buckle and her body sway into his. In one swift movement, he picked her up in his arms, as if she were no heavier than Ellen.

"It is not necessary, my lord . . . I can very well walk," Katherine protested mildly as she let her head fall to his shoulder. She closed her eyes and the world almost disappeared. She felt comforted and safe. She felt his arms tighten around her and gave herself up to the feeling of being protected for the first time since she had arrived at Marston Hall.

Richard held her close. He wanted to erase the preceding ordeal from her memory. She had been so brave. His admiration for her soared. He had never known a woman like her. Gently he carried her to her chamber and laid her on the bed. He stood a moment looking at her pale, exhausted face.

"You're a brave lady, Kate." It was the first time he had called her Kate, or had even thought of her as Kate.

Megan and Lady Amelia bustled into the room in eager concern.

"Let us get this child to bed," Lady Amelia exclaimed. "Megan, bring the water over to the bedstand."

"I will leave her to your good ministrations. But see to it she stays in bed the rest of the day!" Richard ordered. He turned once more to look at her and she opened her eyes to his.

She smiled. Richard's jaw tightened and his hazel-green eyes flashed with emotion for a fleeting moment before the expression disappeared.

"Katherine, there are many to care for Giles today. I order you to rest," he said softly.

Katherine nodded her assent, then closed her eyes.

Amelia and Megan had Katherine comfortably washed and under the covers in a matter of moments. After they silently slipped from the room, Katherine drifted into a deep and healing slumber.

Richard returned briefly to Giles's room. Dr. Deane nodded that all was well as his eyes trailed toward the unconscious patient.

A weariness seemed to seep into Richard's whole being as he continued down the hall. He went downstairs to the library where he went straight to the decanter that held good Napoleon brandy. He poured a generous amount into a delicately cut crystal glass and tossed the contents down his throat. As Richard poured another, he could feel the warmth of the brandy burn his throat and begin to course through his veins. Carrying the glass, he walked over to the large leaded bay window and quietly studied the autumn landscape.

The light streaming through the window cast his face into relief. He was so deep in thought that he did not hear the door open. He was suddenly aware of rustling silk and he turned to find his aunt moving toward him.

"Richard, where are your manners? Do pour one for me," she teased.

"Brandy? Aunt Amelia, I thought a little ratafia or sherry was the most daring drink you ever indulged in." He smiled with a teasing grace.

"Today it is to be brandy!" she replied, characteristically fluttering her ringed fingers.

Richard chuckled as he poured a modest amount for the diminutive lady.

"To Giles's recovery," he said, raising his glass.

"Yes, and to a brave lady," Amelia answered, watching him under veiled lashes.

Richard lowered his eyes but the muscle in his jaw

gave away his tension. "Aye, to that too," he replied, and again drained his glass.

"Did she surprise you, Richard?"

He looked sharply at his aunt, his eyes narrowed in question. He did not answer, but turned and walked to the window again.

"Do you still hold her in disdain, Richard?"

"An adventuress can be courageous. In fact, I suppose it would be a prerequisite," he answered dryly, his defenses immediately raised.

"An adventuress! How vulgar of you!" Her shock could be heard clearly in her voice. She was taken aback at his disdain toward Katherine for she had come to speak to Richard about a far different emotion she feared she had seen in his eyes.

"Vulgar? Everything about Giles is vulgar!" he replied.

"Including his wife? Are you sure that is your feeling about her?" she asked, getting directly to the point she had in mind.

Richard whirled around. "What in the hell do you mean? What are my feelings for my brother's wife?"

"I'd say you are being vulgar now. You need not use profanity to me. I am merely concerned for you. You have been hurt enough and my intentions are merely to warn you to take care lest you find yourself once more in an impossible situation."

"What are you talking about? You asked the question. Speak plainly." His voice now rose in unmasked fury. How many people knew his secret, he wondered.

Amelia knew nothing of Giles's betrayal, only that Richard had been exceedingly unhappy in his previous marriage. "It's just that I've seen your look . . ." She faltered, for now she regretted bringing up the subject. It seemed to distress him so. . . .

"Then, mark it to the romantic novels you read.

Have no fear, my heart is safe from any woman, most of all from the adventuress Giles calls wife!''

Lady Amelia gasped. Her hand flew to her bosom and she stood looking up at her tall nephew. "I believe Shakespeare once said, 'Me thinks, thou dost protest too much.' " She placed her glass on the small inlaid table. "I meant no offense. Just take care, Richard. I know you well, and your heart is not as given freely as Giles's is. You can be hurt. I will say no more. Forgive me."

"It is of no concern. You have not offended me. But rest assured, my heart is safe and sound." With that, he turned his back to her.

Amelia quietly left the room. Richard did not move for a long time.

Chapter 12

The days that followed were remarkable for their sameness. Little changed for Katherine as she and Norton assisted the able Dr. Deane in his careful monitoring of his patient. Giles was certainly no better, but thankfully, he was no worse. He was still in pain and spent long hours sedated so that he would not thrash about and disturb his wounds.

With Dr. Deane in attendance, Katherine had more time for restful pursuits of her own. She began to avail herself of Lord Marston's considerable library. On days the weather permitted she accompanied Ellen on walks or excursions in the garden. She was glad to be able to spend time with the little girl, for it was clear that the child needed some attention. Richard almost never saw his daughter, and on the rare occasions they were together, his indifference toward her was very apparent.

One morning, Katherine decided to take Ellen to the stables to look at the horses. The autumn air was brisk and Katherine smiled down at the bundled little girl whose hand tightly held her own. Ellen's cheeks were rosy and she chattered merrily along as Katherine took dutiful and serious interest in her childish exuberance.

"Sing me the horsey song," Ellen begged as she raised her arms to be picked up.

Kate reached down to pick Ellen up and planted a kiss upon her cheek. "Ride a cockhorse to Banbury Cross—

to see a fine lady upon a white horse. Rings on her fingers and bells on her toes, she shall have music wherever she goes,'' Kate sang merrily and executed a little dance step. She whirled Ellen around and they both laughed and Ellen hugged Katherine's neck tighter.

Katherine looked up to see Lord Marston walking up from the stables, watching them with interest. She halted a moment and Ellen shyly buried her face on Kate's shoulder.

"Good morning, Lord Marston," Kate said with a tentative smile, slightly embarrassed by being observed in her play with Ellen.

He gave a slight nod as he passed them on the stable-yard path and continued on his way without a word.

Katherine, still holding Ellen, slowly turned and watched his retreating figure as he strode manfully toward the manor. She stood transfixed and dumb-founded. He had not spoken, even to Ellen, she thought. The man is as cold as ice! He ignores his own daughter! Kate's cheeks burned with anger, her mind reeling. His feelings toward her are totally lacking! Never had she seen such indifference toward a small child. She pulled Ellen even closer, kissing her a half-dozen times in the few remaining steps to the stables. Great heavens, Kate thought, the child will wither into a lonely girl with no parental attention. Her heart filled with anger and pity on the little girl's behalf. What a monster he was! How could a man be so cold to his own child? she wondered. I shall have to give her what love I can, she vowed, as she continued to shake her head in disbelief.

Katherine held her annoyance at the shocking behavior of Lord Marston throughout the day. She was still fuming with resentment as she dressed for dinner that evening. She knew she would have to be civil to her host but she decided she would be no more than just that.

Dinners were far more interesting to Katherine since Dr. Deane had come to the manor. He enjoyed discussing medical science with her and reminded her of her father and the wonderful conversations they used to have. She looked forward to Dr. Deane's enlightened table discourse as she went downstairs for dinner, vowing to ignore Lord Marston as much as was possible.

Entering the salon, she greeted the Lady Amelia and Dr. Deane with a beaming smile. She gave Lord Marston only a cursory nod. He returned it with a slight rise in his eyebrow and a hint of a frown. Katherine was wearing a charming dress of green taffeta which set off her blue eyes to fine effect. She was feeling rested and her eyes sparkled with suppressed anger. Richard watched her with attentive curiosity.

She paid marked attention to Dr. Deane during dinner and on more than one occasion became so engrossed in his remarks that she fairly ignored Lady Amelia and Richard.

After a particularly spirited debate with the kind doctor, she glanced up to find Richard's eyes resting speculatively on her. Suddenly realizing she had, perhaps, carried her annoyance too far, she blushed like a schoolgirl and quickly lowered her eyes. She knew she had displayed rudeness in her exclusion of Richard; although the act had afforded her pleasure, she realized that she had been rude as well to Lady Amelia, who had done nothing to earn her disregard.

"I beg your pardon. The conversation must be boring to our host and hostess. Dr. Deane, we will continue another time," she said as the doctor nodded in agreement.

"On the contrary," Richard interjected, "I find the conversation most enlightening. We delight in getting to know the scope of Giles's wife's interests, so carry on." He smiled over the wineglass that was poised at his lips.

"Richard," Lady Amelia said, changing the subject, "you must take Katherine to Merrywood. A woman needs to know her home. It will be weeks before Giles can do so and it will be so reassuring to her to finally see her residence. In fact, it might also be diverting, for she might begin to make changes that are needed while Giles recuperates here."

"Aye, it could certainly be arranged. Would you like to do that? Shall we say the day after tomorrow?" he asked.

Katherine paused and put aside her animosity at the thought of the excursion. "Ever so much, especially if we might ride. Is it too far? It has been far too long since I have ridden and I dearly miss doing so," she replied, her face glowing with delight.

Richard took a deep breath. "We shall ride to Merrywood the day after tomorrow, weather permitting." He softly laughed.

"Good," Katherine said with satisfaction. Perhaps, she thought, she might broach the topic of his lack of concern for Ellen. It might be the very opportunity, she mused.

The evening meal continued in the congenial atmosphere with Richard leading the discussion of some modern ideas in farming.

Katherine left the others immediately after dinner and returned to sit next to Giles. He was pale and beginning to look gaunt. There was none of the luster about him that had first attracted her to him. Gone was the humor and charm, for now he lay in a silent world of pain. The hope that had sustained him on his journey to Marston Hall had faded.

Katherine felt his hand and found it was cool. At least there was no fever, she thought, and sat back to rest.

"Lucinda, forgive me," he said in the barest whisper of words.

Katherine looked up sharply and rose to stand beside him.

"Giles, it is I, Katherine. Do you want anything? Something to drink?" she asked. He did not answer, for he had slipped into unconsciousness again. She stood perfectly still. Why did he call for Lucinda? A little shiver ran up her spine, and suddenly, all she wanted to do was leave.

Katherine went to the hall and called one of the servants. "Please inform the marquess that I have retired. See to it that he has someone sit with Giles now. I am unable to," she instructed, then hastily made her way to her own room.

She excused Megan immediately and closed the door, for she needed time alone. She slipped off her gown and undergarments, leaving them exactly where she had stepped out of them. Her hands shook slightly as she slowly donned her nightgown and robe. Taking down her hair, she sat by the crackling fire, brushing the long curls, unable to dispel her feeling of uneasiness. When at last she slipped into bed, some of the vague, disturbed feelings began to abate. For the first time in weeks, she drifted into sleep without thinking of Giles.

The next morning, Richard sent word they would leave early for Merrywood. Nora helped Katherine into the fetching riding habit she had worn the day she and Giles had first ridden along the coast at Dover.

"Do hurry, Nora, for I must see how Giles is before I leave," she said excitedly as the maid finished pinning on her hat. Glancing in the mirror, Kate smoothed down her skirt and hurriedly left the room.

"Giles, good morning!" she said as she entered her husband's chamber. "It's a lovely day! How are you feeling?" she asked, her excitement at the impending outing unmasked.

Pale and drawn, he lay watching her cross the room, an expression of displeasure on his face. "I see you are in fine spirits . . . about to gallivant across the countryside. With whom? Richard?" he asked with glittering eyes.

"Yes, he is taking me to see Merrywood. I'm delighted," she happily replied. "I'll certainly enjoy the ride as well as seeing our future home."

Giles leveled a harsh look upon her radiant face. "You are to be commended. While I lie here, you cavort with Richard across the countryside."

The uneasy feeling of the previous night returned. "Would you rather I did not go?" she quietly said as the happy expression faded from her face. "Giles . . . I do not understand. You object?"

"Hell, yes. You belong here with me," he snapped.

Norton, who had been quietly watching the exchange, began to rise from his seat. "Missy, you go. I'll stay with him. You need a change of scene. You've sat here beside this bed far too much."

Katherine was not the least disturbed by Norton's intervention, but Giles's face became distorted in rage. "Get out! I don't want you here. Go, go! Make calf eyes at Richard if you wish. Your forever cheerful chatter drives me mad. Go. Now!" he spat.

Katherine gasped. Her hand flew to her lips. She turned on her heel. "Giles, you wouldn't know care and concern when it is given. I'll not stay, nor return until your disposition changes. Let me know if and when you wish to see me," she said as she rushed from the room with tears brimming in her eyes.

Norton turned to Giles. "Ye'll not ever speak to Miss Katherine that way again," he said with a menace that brooked no reply.

Richard watched her as she crossed the stone yard, gracefully holding her skirt and exposing her soft black half boots. Her hat sat jauntily on her head and the black feathers curled along her cheek in sharp contrast to her creamy white skin. Her clear blue eyes were enhanced by the sapphire-blue habit. Richard took in every detail of her appearance and felt a constriction in his chest.

Immediately, he noted her distress. He reached out and touched her arm. "Is something wrong?" he asked softly. His green-flecked eyes searched her face. She raised eyes still smarting with tears and said, "Yes, but I'm quite all right. It is just Giles . . . he is out of sorts. He told me to get out . . ." She sighed, then suddenly regretted her words.

Richard swore a soft oath. He wanted to protect her suddenly. Placing his gloved hand along her cheek, he tenderly smiled. "Let us put it aside for now. The day is lovely and you deserve an outing. Giles will come around later," he said, doubting his own words, for he knew Giles far too well. Katherine returned a tentative smile and nodded. When he heard the clacking of hooves, he reluctantly let his hand drop.

The groom led over two horses which had already been saddled. Richard's mount was a powerful black stallion and Katherine's was a spirited chestnut with a white star on its forehead. She smiled, for it reminded her of her own horse back in Dover.

"What lovely horses! Tell me their names," she said, trying to throw off her tense mood. Walking over to her mount, she took the bridle in her hand and patted the horse's soft silky nose while cooing soft compliments to it.

"Mine is Taranis. He's named for a Celtic God whose name means thunder. Yours is Marigold," he replied with an amused expression.

"Marigold? Such a prosaic name for such an elegant horse. It doesn't seem to suit her." She laughed.

"It is a legacy of her wayward youth. She had a passion for marigolds and ate whole borders of them to the dismay of the irate gardeners. She still succumbs to their apparent culinary appeal whenever possible," he explained.

"Indeed; well, Marigold, let us see how well you ride." She laughed as she allowed the groom to help her into the saddle.

Richard swung up into his saddle and urged Taranis out of the gates of the courtyard. Katherine followed.

After the many days spent cooped up in the sick room, the ride was exhilarating. Katherine's spirits soared with each mile that they cantered over the sun-swept countryside in the crisp morning air. They rode at a brisk pace so little conversation was exchanged.

Katherine thought Richard sat his horse well and looked exceedingly handsome. There is something about a handsome man who sits a horse well, she thought, smiling. Rather like there is something about a man in uniform, she mused as she turned to look at him. He met her gaze and returned a smile that indicated he was enjoying the ride as much as she.

After a half hour, they rode through two brick gates and down a long drive from which they could see Merrywood. It was a charming house which had been built in 1700 during the reign of William and Mary. Its red-brick walls, sash windows, and hip roof indicated the Dutch influence of that era. It was built in the old traditional H plan of the Elizabethan era but its design was decidedly Palladian. Graceful half columns supported the large pediment on the central bay. The house was not monumental but much larger than Katherine had envisioned. The name, Merrywood, had somehow indicated to her a far more modest home.

"Richard, it is lovely. Far grander than I had supposed," she exclaimed as he reached up to help her from the saddle. His hands spanned her slender waist and she flushed as they seemed to linger there after setting her to the ground. She turned her head to avoid his eyes and looked at the entrance of the house.

Just then the door opened and the butler appeared. "Good day to you, Lord Marston," he said formally. His eyes traveled to the beautiful young woman he knew to be his new mistress.

"Mrs. Swynford, I should like to present Vernon to you. He is Merrywood's butler, and a most capable one."

"Thank you for your kind words, my lord," Vernon smiled and turned to offer Katherine a bow. "It is indeed an honor. We welcome a new mistress and will do all to make your new home a pleasure to reside in."

They entered the richly paneled entrance hall and Katherine was delightfully surprised at the magnificent paintings that were hung there. A previous owner had obviously loved quality artworks.

Richard introduced her to the housekeeper, Mrs. Greeves, who was a tall, slender woman with a neat, efficient appearance.

"Mrs. Swynford, we are delighted to have a new mistress. Our prayers are with Captain Swynford for his speedy recovery. We are so anxious to have a family in residence again. 'Tis a lovely house and we wish you much happiness in it," she said, bobbing with a curtsy.

"Thank you, Mrs. Greeves. My husband is improving and we hope his recovery will allow us to move in soon," Katherine replied.

Richard took her arm and began to lead her through the house. Katherine was delighted with its light airy rooms. The house did seem somewhat neglected but she thought new fabrics and paint would easily correct all that.

Richard was very cordial as he suggested various improvements. He explained the house was built on an extensive property and that Giles was fortunate to have an excellent bailiff. He told her the estate was profitable.

"I hope Giles can be happy now," Richard commented as they entered the long gallery.

"Why do you say that? Has he not been happy here?" she asked.

Richard looked down into her wide blue eyes and for a moment was unable to comment. "Well, now he has you, and that should make the difference," he replied a bit dryly.

Katherine returned his gaze and a spark seemed to pass between them as they stood looking at one another for a moment. Then Richard took her arm to guide her to the upper chambers. His hand seemed to burn through her sleeve and she lowered her eyes.

They entered the master bedroom, which was dominated by a huge bed.

"This is the master chamber. It has a beautiful view of the small lake." Richard spoke softly with a trace of rancor in his voice. For some reason he could not understand, the vision of Giles and Katherine together in the bed brought a stab of pain to his heart. He hastily put the thought from his mind.

"Let us examine the stables before we have luncheon," he quickly suggested.

As they toured the stables, she was pleased with the sturdy buildings and well-kept stalls. But it was the fine horseflesh Giles owned, that sent her into raptures. She stopped frequently to pet the handsome animals, cooing tender words to them with a gentle expression on her face.

"They are wonderful horses. Giles never mentioned he had such a fine stable!" she exclaimed.

"Aye, he has a good eye, indeed," Richard replied as he turned to look at Katherine. He absentmindedly raised his hand to brush a stray tendril of hair from her cheek. When Katherine almost jumped with surprise, Richard frowned and turned his steps toward the house.

"Luncheon will be ready. Then we must return to Marston," he commented as his stride quickly lengthened. Katherine had to fairly fly to keep up with him.

Richard seemed unusually jovial during luncheon that day. He regaled Katherine with stories of his and Giles's boyhood escapades.

"I was forever pulling Giles out of one scrape after another. At least the ones he couldn't charm his way out of. And he was quite often able to do that. Did he ever tell you about the time it snowed up instead of down?" He chuckled.

"Up? You mean from the ground up?"

"Aye, 'tis true. The wind off the North Sea blew with such force that when it hit the land it swirled the snow upward for hours. One couldn't see two feet ahead. Giles was so excited he bundled up and went off into the storm. It took us two hours to find him and he was fairly frozen when we did. My mother was sick with worry, but Giles just laughed at his lark. He was enthralled."

Katherine laughed. She was seeing a side of Richard she had never seen before, and she liked it. She looked up to find Richard's eyes resting on her.

"It's good to see you laugh, Kate," he said softly as he rose from the table. "But now, we must return to Marston."

"Yes, I'm sure we must," she replied. Gracious, she thought, how nice it would be to stay. . . .

Chapter 13

Katherine rose early the next morning feeling happy. For no particular reason, she hummed to herself as she donned a very pretty apricot dress. It was tied high under her bosom with Prussian-blue ribbons and had puffed sleeves trimmed with the same ribbon. Megan piled her hair on top of her head and wove more blue ribbon through her curls. After an appreciative glance at her reflection, Katherine picked up a shawl to carry and jauntily left the room.

Though her duties caring for Giles had been greatly reduced with Dr. Deane in residence, she made her way down the hall to her husband's bedchamber to see how he progressed. Entering the room, she found both Richard and Dr. Deane with Giles. His eyes met hers as she crossed over to the bed.

"How is Giles this morning?" she asked.

Her husband smiled up and weakly offered her his hand. As she took it, her feeling of gaiety quickly faded.

"How are you, Kate?" he asked in a faint voice.

"At least you don't mistake me for Lucinda today. So you must be better," she innocently replied, trying to hold on to her feeling of lighter humor.

Richard's eyes narrowed. He wondered how much she knew.

A pained look came over Giles's face. "You must discount the ramblings of a sick man, Kate," he said.

An ominous silence fell over the room.

"Of course I do, Giles. I was just teasing you. Now that you recognize me, I shall have to stop nagging you to eat, lest you get out of sorts with me," she bantered.

Giles smiled weakly. "Aye, 'tis a nagging wife I have, but a beautiful one."

Katherine was grateful to see a little spark of his old light-hearted charm return.

"We are pleased with his progress. He's doing well," Dr. Deane interjected.

"Excellent." She turned back to her husband. "Shall I read for you awhile?"

"Another time, Kate. My mind is too full of feathers to listen. I shall just rest so that we can ride the moors together soon," he replied.

Kate paused a moment. "Then I shall take Ellen for a walk. The days grow cooler and we won't be able to enjoy such excursions much longer."

"I should like to see Ellen if you would please bring her to me for a moment before you go," Giles said, his voice fading.

Richard, who had been leaning up against the mantelpiece, straightened up suddenly with a cold expression in his eyes.

"Indeed, I shall bring her directly to you," Kate answered as she left to do his bidding.

"If you will excuse me, there are matters for me to attend," Richard said curtly, and also made to leave. He and Katherine entered the corridor at the same time. Puzzled by his curt manner, she gave him a curious look.

At Katherine's request, Nanny Burke bundled Ellen in warm clothing. The little girl skipped with happiness and chattered excitedly with Katherine as she went to see her Uncle Giles.

Giles's face lit with a smile as he watched their

sprightly entrance. Katherine thought it was the sweetest smile she had seen since the day he had proposed.

"Come say hello to your uncle, Ellen. My, but you've grown to be such a pretty little girl," he called fondly.

Ellen advanced a little shyly and returned his smile.

How like her uncle she is, thought Katherine. She had never noticed it before, but with her pale golden-brown eyes and dimples Ellen was the very image of Giles. Of course, Giles looked much like Richard except for his coloring. Richard had so much green in his eyes, Katherine mused.

They did not stay long, for Katherine did not want to tire Giles and Ellen was eager to go find some pretty leaves, as she explained to her uncle.

"Bring some pretty leaves to me, Ellen. I can't get them myself this year but next we'll go together," Giles said as he closed his eyes to sleep. He seemed content.

The outing proved to be successful for Ellen found more beautifully colored leaves than they could carry. With rosy cheeks and sparkling eyes, Kate and Ellen returned, laughing, to the hall.

A fine carriage was parked outside the front entrance, and when they entered the front hall, they found Richard talking to a beautiful woman dressed in the most elegant fashion. A tall, regal woman with a slender, aristocratic face, she was dressed in a white muslin gown with a pale blue pelisse and wore a large blue bonnet made of shirred silk and white feathers.

Richard smiled at the merry entrance of Katherine and Ellen and noted their healthy glow.

"Katherine, may I present Lady Hampton to you. Cornelia, I should like to introduce you to my brother's wife, Mrs. Swynford," he said.

Cornelia Hampton coolly surveyed the beautiful woman before her and did not like what she saw.

Cornelia was well used to being the reigning beauty in most gatherings and did not take kindly to competition.

Putting a proprietary hand on the marquess's arm, she greeted Katherine in a rather condescending manner. "It is so nice that you are able to stay here while Giles recovers. I do hope he is getting on. With your help, I'm sure he is." She smiled appropriately.

My, my, my, thought Katherine, Richard has certainly wasted no time in telling her all about me. This annoyed her and she flashed him a quelling look.

Richard raised an eyebrow in surprise. What in the devil has set her off, he wondered.

"Papa, look! Leaves! Aunt Kate and I found them! Here's one for you." Ellen offered one of her precious finds to her father.

Richard looked down at the pretty child whose hand was outstretched with her slightly rumpled gift. He glanced at Katherine momentarily and saw her watching him with interest.

"Thank you, Ellen," he stiffly replied as he bent to receive the offering.

Lady Hampton, who did not like to be out of the center of things for even a moment, immediately exclaimed, "How charming she is, Richard."

Katherine smiled inwardly, thinking Lady Hampton did not look like the kind of woman who would, for one moment, risk mussing her elegant dress with the grubby hands of a child. So with a rather perverse motive and a decided twinkle in her eye, Kate bent down and picked the child up. A shower of gold and red leaves fell to the floor as Ellen put her arms about Katherine's neck.

"Bid Lady Hampton and your papa good-bye. It's time for luncheon," she said to Ellen, then turned and added, "it was a pleasure to meet you. Good day."

"Yes, thank you. I'm sure we'll meet again. Give my regards to Giles and tell him I should like to visit him when he is feeling better and lonely for some company.

I've just returned from London and have all the latest *on-dits*. He'll find them very amusing, I'm sure," Lady Hampton replied as she smiled her best *beau monde* smile.

Katherine nodded and turned to carry Ellen up the staircase.

"Katherine, do join us for luncheon," Richard called after her.

"Thank you, but I shall eat with Giles," she said without looking back.

Katherine heard Lady Hampton's voice give a tinkling laugh as she exclaimed, "What a delight it shall be to have a visit with you, Richard; it has been simply ages since I have seen you."

As Katherine entered Giles's bedchamber, Dr. Deane rose to greet her. "Mrs. Swynford, I am pleased with his progress today. If he continues to improve at the same rate, I shall leave before the week is out."

"We would be sorry to see you leave, for you have done us a great service. However, it could not but be a happy event, for Giles would then be well on the mend," she replied graciously.

Dr. Deane smiled with the well-earned satisfaction of a job well done, then took his leave to join Richard for luncheon.

"Are not you going to dine with them?" Giles asked.

"No, since you are so alert, I shall take pleasure in your company." She smiled sweetly as she seated herself in her usual chair. "I've arranged to have luncheon with you. Perhaps I can convince you to eat more so you can regain your strength," she continued.

Giles watched her under carefully hooded eyes, like a cat ready to prey on an unsuspecting bird. "You seem exceptionally cheerful. How goes it with Richard?" he asked.

"How goes what with Richard?" she returned, slightly perplexed by the question.

"How do you two get on?" he pressed.

Katherine leveled him a direct look. "Passable. Frankly, Giles, I cannot say I care much for him. Still, he has been most kind and helpful in providing the aid for your recovery."

"I'll not place a wager on that," he said dryly.

"Why, whatever do you mean? He sent for Dr. Deane," she argued in Richard's defense.

"Seems as though you are exceedingly anxious to become his champion," he continued, malice glittering in his eyes.

"You're just out of sorts because you are bored from your long confinement. Of course, he has been helpful, and well you know it . . . He hasn't been exactly cheerful, I will admit, but it doesn't seem to be his way with you," she replied, just a bit annoyed. "However, I am perplexed at just how little attention he gives his daughter. I fear he is basically an unfeeling man," she continued.

"My, my, you learn fast, Kate, but don't underestimate him. He cares not for Ellen, to be sure, but loves only his precious Marston and his cows and pigs."

Katherine laughed at this remark. "Giles, you're as cross as a wild boar! Would you like me to read to you? Perhaps I can change your sour mood."

"Sour is it? You'd be sour if you were confined to a bed while your brother made calf eyes at your wife!" he retorted with surprising vehemence.

"Giles! How unkind! 'Tis not so, and well you know it. He doesn't even like me! He almost seems to resent me," she replied. "In fact, this conversation is so ridiculous, I shall not continue it. Let us read or play cribbage. Which is it?" she said with finality in her voice.

"Read," he said listlessly. He rested his head back on his pillows with a low moan.

"Giles, are you well? What is troubling you? Let me help." She reached for his hand.

"Leave me, Kate. My devils haunt me today. I'll be more the thing, later . . ." His voice trailed off.

She rose, stood a moment, and watched him. Who was he? What did she know of him? He was so different from the charming, romantic suitor she had met back in Dover. Ah, well, who can blame him? He will be himself again when he is fit once more. No one could remain carefree after these months of illness, she mused.

Studying him, Katherine frowned. There was a harsh line around his mouth lately that truly perplexed her. A nagging uncertain intuition that Giles was not all she had supposed he was had been slowly creeping into her thoughts. She denied what she termed "disloyal" thoughts, and forced them from her mind, refusing to examine them.

Now she was a little frightened. Where was the happy carefree Giles who had managed the most difficult part of their journey? Since their arrival, he had changed. It was as if he lay in wait for something, but what? She shrugged her slender shoulders. It was just the illness, she told herself.

She was about to leave when a maid brought her tray into the room. She asked that it be taken to her own room, for she longed for some peace and quiet. After lunch, she sat at the delicate inlaid writing table in her room and penned a long missive to her father.

Her words revealed more unrest than she ever intended, and the letter was later to be read with alarm by the astute Dr. Spencer, who knew his daughter well. He ran his hand along his chin in dismay as he read the hidden distress in her words. He decided it was time he paid a visit to Northumberland.

Chapter 14

Richard watched Katherine as she entered the breakfast room. His eyes lit up with a soft glow that went unnoticed by Katherine as she bid good morning to Lady Amelia.

The look was duly noted by Amelia and she slightly shook her head in dismay as she turned to acknowledge Katherine's greeting.

"Good morning, my dear. My, it may be October but you look like spring sunshine in your yellow. It is a joy to behold how you lighten this solemn hall," Amelia gushed in genuine affection.

"Why, thank you, Amelia. You are too kind." Katherine playfully feigned a gesture of modesty and dropped an exaggerated curtsy.

Even the solemn Richard smiled, as did the two attending footmen, who struggled to retain their usual austere expressions.

"Good morning, Lord Marston. And how are all the chickens and cows?" she teased, eyeing his fine-fitting buckskins. "You must have ridden out early to be back so soon," Kate said.

"Aye, I was up early. Sleep seemed to evade me in the wee hours of the morning. It is an exceptional morning. Would you like to ride? You will delight in the day, I assure you. One of the last days of autumn I believe, for there is a sharp crispness in the air that hints at winter."

"Twice in one morning? You'll sleep tonight with so much exercise, I'll wager. Yes, I should love to ride out this morning. Nanny can care for Ellen," Katherine replied as she accepted a plate of kippers, baked tomatoes, muffins, and marmalade from the liveried footman.

Lord Marston raised an eyebrow. "Indeed, that is Nanny's post. You take too much on . . ."

"It helps to pass the time. Times seems to hang heavy on my hands lately," she replied.

"Katherine, if it were not for our circumstance, we could give a ball . . . That would cheer you up!" Amelia lightheartedly suggested, feeling a pang of regret that such an event would not take place.

Katherine laughed. "I have only been to one real ball, so I could not say."

"You do not mean it. Great heavens, child." Amelia gasped in amazement. "When all is right again—when we are out of mourning, and Giles is fit, we shall give the most elegant ball the north has seen in many a year. My, how I do miss going about." She sighed. "Which reminds me, Richard, as soon as Giles is out of danger, I shall return to Bath. I do miss my friends and all."

"Yes, of course. I understand. We shall miss your cheerful company, for the Lord knows we need you . . ." His voice trailed off.

Amelia smiled at his compliment, but declined to reply. It was time she returned to her own household. She did not really feel needed any longer with Katherine here. She had come to be with Richard at Lucinda's death, and would leave as soon as Giles was up and about a little.

After changing into her riding habit, Katherine met Richard in the courtyard. The horses were saddled and the groomsmen held them in waiting. Richard himself assisted Katherine into the saddle. She could feel his warm breath on her cheek as he moved closer to help her, and his nearness made her avert her eyes from his.

Watching him swing up into the saddle, Katherine could not help but admire his athletic grace. He turned his head and nodded as he directed his horse through the stone archway and along the pathway that led to the parkland. He smiled in her direction and Katherine realized he shared her excitement as she followed his lead.

They lengthened the strides of the horses and raced through the golden sea of oaks and out into the open, rolling meadows.

"Oh, Richard it is beautiful," she exclaimed as she turned her face, shining with animation, to him. Her eyes were as blue as the October sky, and they shone with a happiness he had not seen before.

Richard's hands tightened on the reins and the great stallion tossed his head. "Aye, beautiful," he replied. He turned away, as he felt a pang of longing in his chest. Damn Giles, he never should have brought her here.

They came to rest on a summit of one of the rolling hills. Richard sat a moment, viewing the far-reaching vista. Life at this summit seemed eternal, as if it would go on forever . . . .

As Katherine watched his handsome profile, a breeze ruffled his brown curls and his hair caught highlights of fire from the sun. At that instant he seemed bigger than life, as if he might will the world to his way. She smiled at her silly fancy. Suddenly, he became conscious of her, and turned to meet her gaze. His hazel eyes glinted with the flashes of green in the sunlight. He froze in his saddle, as if suspended in time.

As they looked into each other's eyes and saw the undisguised emotion there, a sudden shock of understanding went through them.

Richard longed to reach out for her but quickly

quelled the stirring of his quickened heart. He turned his head to hide his raw expression, and when he again returned his gaze, it was cool and impersonal.

Katherine felt an electric thrill course through her body. It left her feeling helpless and frightened. She turned away and, with pounding heart, said, "I must return to Giles."

When she looked up at his now-cold expression, she met it with one that was equally remote.

Later, Katherine could not remember how she had managed to get through the rest of the day. It seemed to last forever. She was shaken beyond belief. How had this happened, she asked herself. How could she possibly be drawn to Richard? She could not bring herself to answer that question.

When the day had finally ended she stood alone in her chamber. Thank God it's over, she thought. But there was still tomorrow.

Katherine remembered how closely Giles had questioned her on her obvious preoccupation that afternoon and she had fled, pleading a headache. She chided herself for being a coward.

Staring at her reflection, she saw her large blue eyes were glowing with a secret light. Oh God, she cried to herself, and buried her face in her trembling hands. It shows, she acknowledged. She wept.

When at last her tears subsided, she raised her head. The only sound in the room was the ticking of the clock and the soft crash of a falling log on the grate. She was so alone.

As if to banish the devils that haunted her, she furiously began to brush her hair. She quickly plaited it, as if that action might bring order to the sudden chaos in her life. She rose and removed her soft emerald velvet robe and slipped into bed.

Richard had filled his day with furious activity, so he would have no time to think. Dinner had been a living hell. All he had wanted to do was look at Katherine and therefore he never did. He had eaten without much conversation and then excused himself.

Now he sat in the library, brandy in hand, and his long booted legs stretched out before the fireplace. His strong slender fingers toyed with his glass. His brows were brought together in a deep frown. He would overcome this feeling, he rationalized. He had to. There were no other avenues open to him.

Sleep would not come and Katherine began to toss as her agitation grew. Finally, she threw back the covers. She reached for her robe and tied it about her waist, swinging the long braid down her back. She found her slippers, picked up a shielded taper, and left her room.

She decided to find something to read. Perhaps, she thought, that would help her fall asleep. Some philosophical tome would do perfectly, she reasoned as her quiet steps carried her down the darkened corridors and staircase into the library.

Slumped in his chair, Richard heard the door softly open. He knew it was Katherine—how he knew he could not fathom—but he knew. He did not move but listened to the soft rustle of fabric and light footsteps as she crossed the room to the stacks.

She carried a taper which cast a soft glow on her beautiful face. She did not see him. He watched her and smiled when he saw the prim braid, for he remembered the tumbled mass of hair about her shoulders the first time he had laid eyes on her.

Katherine reached for a book, but paused in midair. He was here, she knew, just knew! She slowly turned and found his glittering eyes upon her. She couldn't move. The shock of awareness reverberated once more between them. Richard slowly rose and placed his glass upon the small wine table. Katherine stood rooted, her heart pounding.

He advanced slowly toward her, the firelight casting

his figure along the wall and ceiling as it had the first
night he had met her. Towering over her, he stood
before her, taking in the glowing beauty of her face that
had never been far from his memory in days. He read
the poignant look in her eyes. She appeared so
vulnerable and lost. He reached up and took the candle
holder from her hand and placed it on the table without
saying a word.

He reached out for her and pulled her to him. She
could feel the strength in the hard muscles of his chest
and the arms encircling her waist. His arms tightened
around her as his head came down and his mouth
covered hers.

Katherine trembled as he kissed her softly, his mouth
warm with the taste of brandy. Her arms slid up around
his neck and he pulled her even closer. Their bodies
pressed together. His arms tightened around her as his
tongue probed her soft, willing mouth. His hand slid
slowly down her back, and he pressed her hips to his.
She could feel his obvious arousal and her blood seemed
to turn to fire in her veins. She entered a world she had
never traveled before and the tingling, thrilling sensa-
tions were wondrous, delicious. All else faded and only
her increasing need to be close to him remained.

Richard untied her belt and his hand slid up to cup
one of her soft, round breasts. She trembled as his
thumb slowly circled her nipple until it became taut
against his hand. His kisses trailed along her throat; she
could feel his warm breath on her neck and shoulder.
He pulled her gown aside and kissed her well-rounded
breasts.

Her hand moved to his head and she slipped her
fingers through the rich thickness of his hair.

"Katherine, Katherine," he tenderly murmured,
"why aren't you mine?" He covered her mouth and
eyes with kisses. "I've needed you since I first laid eyes

on you. Katherine . . ." His voice was smothered in renewed kisses.

I'm lost, she thought as he slid her gown and robe from her shoulders and the garments tumbled to the floor.

He picked her up and carried her to the large settee and laid her down, taking in her creamy beauty. Her arms went up around his neck and he bent once more to kiss her.

A sound of footsteps in the hall made Richard's head snap up. He stiffened. He let Katherine go so swiftly she suddenly felt the cold air wash over her. He silently strode to the door of the library which was still slightly ajar, snapped it shut, and turned the heavy brass key. He stood a moment and looked toward her.

Sense and fear gripped Katherine. She felt overwhelmingly vulnerable and shame rushed through her.

Slowly he returned to her, his eyes glittering with passion, and he reached once more for her.

Katherine rose and began to fumble back into her nightdress. "Richard, no, we can't . . . I mean I—oh Richard," she softly cried, tears brimming up in her enormous glowing eyes.

He paused, his heart pounding. His need was almost beyond control, yet he paused. They stood a moment while Katherine fumbled into her robe. Then anger slowly gripped Richard, more toward himself than toward Kate.

"God, what am I about?" he mumbled in disbelief.

"I know, we can't. I should not be here! It is wrong, horribly wrong!" she cried.

"Then why the hell are you here?" he spat in frustration. His harshness took her by surprise.

"I came for a book. I did not expect to find you here, least of all that we'd . . ." Her voice faded as embarrassment and chagrin began to fill her.

He looked away. He longed to take her—here, now. He could and he knew it. Her tears didn't fool him; she was just like Lucinda—ready to fall into the bed of another man without a thought for her husband. Damn, he thought, and turned his fiery eyes to her once more. She stood before him, shaking.

"As I have said before, if you can't have one brother, you'll have the other," he derided, his frustration causing him to speak bitterly.

Katherine gasped. "How could you? Richard—" She raised her hand to touch him.

Richard swept her an elegant bow. "Good night, my lady adventuress."

The hand that had reached out moments ago in tenderness to touch him now swung a resounding slap against his cheek. Since he was still in the motion of bending, her blow almost knocked him over.

"Adventuress! How dare you! You, Lord Marston, who would cuckold your own brother!"

Richard stood and watched as she fumbled with the key and then let herself out of the door. He did not move. His eyes glittered with passion and contempt.

Chapter 15

Richard stood silent and shocked. Carried away by his longing and desire for Katherine, he had behaved in a manner of which he had never thought himself capable. He was a man of honor, and now he stood totally aghast at his weakness and the extravagance of his betrayal.

Insight into the liaison between Giles and Lucinda struck him with full force. How he had resented them these last years. Even innocent Ellen had suffered from his bitterness, for he had never accepted her as a daughter. Every time he saw the child he thought of Giles's betrayal, so he chose to ignore her just as he had Lucinda. Now he found himself to be no more honorable than his weak, selfish brother. Richard was devastated.

Remembering his cruel words to Katherine and the hurt in her eyes, he realized the damage he had done. He bowed his head in remorse and vowed to correct, as much as possible, the injury he had inflicted.

After leaving the library, Katherine fled to her room. She closed the door and leaned against it as if to hold all the world at bay. A world that was shattered. Her beliefs, her faith in herself and others lay like broken glass at her feet. Tears streamed down her cheeks. She leaned her head against the door and wondered. Was she just what Richard thought her to be? How had this happened? Only the noise of a servant checking locks on the doors, which interrupted their lovemaking, had saved her from giving herself to Richard. How had she fallen in love with Giles's brother? She was a moral and honest woman, but she had behaved no better than a common strumpet. She flung herself upon the bed and wept until there were no more tears.

The following days were difficult. Katherine and Richard avoided one another on every possible occasion. The evening meals were the greatest trial. Richard extended himself in conversation to Amelia and Katherine in what he hoped was a normal manner. Katherine was equally polite, responding with frequent smiles, just as if nothing had happened and all was well.

Lady Amelia observed the haunted looks and restrained manner between them, and while she could not fathom what was wrong, she knew something was. This worried her.

If Katherine seemed somewhat preoccupied to the servants, it could be attributed to Giles's failing health. His first rally had begun to fade and now he seemed to linger listlessly.

When Katherine entered Giles's bedchamber one morning she found him pale and weak.

"Good morning, Giles," Kate cheerfully greeted him.

He turned his head and smiled, "Ah, faithful Kate. You must be sorely tried to be tied to a dying man."

Katherine's heart skipped a beat. Did he know? she thought guiltily. She had prayed and prayed for his recovery. She vowed to be the best wife a man could possibly have if only he would get better.

In the guilt over her feelings for Richard, she failed to recognize that she had been a good wife. She had stood behind him on the arduous journey to Marston Hall and nursed him for months in his illness. Her marriage had never been consummated and therefore the normal affection she should feel for a husband simply did not have the opportunity to grow. Nor was she aware of Giles's true feelings or the real reason he had married her.

"Giles, you are getting better every day. Soon you will be fit and we will ride the moors together as you have promised. I hold you to that pledge," she lied.

He smiled wanly and shook his head. "Kate, I have done you an injustice. I never should have married you and brought you here."

"Giles, do not say that is so. We will make a happy marriage, I promise you," she cried in desperation, her hidden guilt carried in every word.

"No, Kate. You do not deserve what I have done to you. You're young and beautiful and should have a husband who loves you," he replied softly.

"You don't love me, Giles?"

"I've never loved anyone. My life has been one only of envy and revenge for what could not be mine . . ." He turned his face from her, his lips tight and blue.

"Why did you marry me?" she asked as her heart began to pound in her chest.

"To make Richard jealous. I knew the minute I met you, you would be the woman for him."

"Jealous, why would you want that?" she asked in a bare whisper.

"I wanted to have something he could not have," Giles said, "and you, angel, were to be the one thing he could not own."

Silence followed his confession, for Katherine could think of no reply. In fact, she did not understand exactly what he was trying to tell her. She sat with her trembling hands in her lap.

"Oh, Giles, you were wrong to bring me here. You never should have." She wept.

"Aye, and I now beg your forgiveness," he whispered, and turned anguished eyes to her.

"You'll have Merrywood, Kate. And see to Ellen, for Richard does not love her."

"Giles, you speak as if you're not going to live, but you will. We'll manage, I promise, even if you don't love me."

"No, Kate, I'm dying and I know it. In fact I welcome death. Life has been my hell. I've always hated my position. I've always hated Richard with his imperious ways. I should have been the first son. I love Marston Hall and would have been a better marquess."

"But you have Merrywood. It is beautiful. You could be happy there. Try Giles, try and live. We'll be happy!" She was openly weeping now.

"No, Kate, never. I only ask your forgiveness, as I must ask others before I die. Now, leave me, please."

"I forgive you, Giles," she said between sobs. But she did not. She was angry, not because of his lack of love but because of the position in which he had placed her. She rose and softly left the room. Giles did not call her back.

Once more, Katherine took to the sanctuary of her room. It was the only place where she could be comfortable and alone. After dismissing Megan, claiming she was not well and wished to be alone, she paced the room. Her nerves were raw and shocked with emotion. Dear Lord, she prayed, help me through this morass. Give me the strength to get through this nightmare so that I may return to Dover and Father. Finally, exhaustion overwhelmed her and she lay down upon the bed. Sleep, escaping sleep, overcame her and she drifted in and out of troubled dreams.

Downstairs, Richard wondered about the whereabouts of Katherine to Lady Amelia at luncheon.

"I do not know where she is either, Richard. I am worried about her. She is troubled. Giles is not doing well and I fear the strain is beginning to show," Amelia said as she carefully observed her nephew.

She watched a concerned expression cross his face, then fade behind his usual imperturbable mask. A muscle twitched in his jaw, the only visible sign of any reaction to her remark.

"Richard! You are too hard on the young woman. She has been nothing but devoted to Giles. You must see to her welfare. It is your duty," she innocently instructed.

Richard did not answer. He finished his meal in silence. When he rose to excuse himself, he said, "I shall inquire as to her welfare, as you suggest."

Lord Marston sought out Megan and asked, "How is your mistress? She did not appear for luncheon. Is she well?" His voice revealed his concern.

"No, my lord, she is not. She sat with Captain Swynford this morning and has returned to her room. I am concerned, for she would not have me assist her," she replied, dropping him a curtsy.

"Thank you, Megan. I shall look in on her." His harsh face gave Megan the chills and she stood watching him stride to the staircase and purposefully mount the steps.

Richard knocked softly on Katherine's door. He received no reply. He turned the large brass handle, entered the room, and saw Katherine on the bed. The sound of the knocking had entered Kate's consciousness and caused her to stir and partially awaken.

Her hair had come unpinned and the mass of dark curls framed the oval face, just as it had the night he first met her. He watched her for a moment, wanting to cradle her in his arms, to comfort her. He dismissed the desire immediately.

Katherine slowly opened her eyes and sleepily became aware that Richard was standing beside her. The softness of sleep surrounded her in a comforting haze and she fleetingly smiled. The smile quickly disappeared when the reality of his presence set in.

"What do you want, my lord?" she asked curtly.

"To inquire as to how you fare, my lady," he replied in an even voice. Its soft resonance sent a shiver down her back. He smiled that infuriating, wonderful smile.

"You forgot 'Adventuress,' Lord Marston."

"Katherine, forgive me for that. I was angry at myself. It was unforgiveable, but I ask forgiveness."

"Hardly, my lord. Please leave. I am no concern of yours," she snapped.

"Are you sure you are well? Can I see to anything you might wish?" he continued.

"Lord Marston, do I not make myself clear? You can do nothing for me. You have done quite enough already. I understand Giles's abhorrence of you all too well. Now leave!" Katherine's blue eyes brimmed with tears, for the events of the day were beyond a saint's patience.

Richard started to touch her cheek but checked the motion. "Very well, but do not hesitate to call anyone for what you might wish," he said with a sadness in his voice.

As he turned to leave he paused once more. "Kate, forgive me."

Katherine lay quietly for several moments after the door had softly shut. Could she ever forgive him? she wondered. But it was not him she needed to forgive. It was her own self and that would not come easy. Now, however, she knew Giles had never really loved her. She realized that was why her own caring had died so quickly and why, perhaps, she had been so vulnerable to the handsome Lord Marston. She instinctively knew he was by far the finer man, despite his overt sexual interest in her.

Richard traversed the hall and entered Giles's room. Norton, a chambermaid, and Dr. Deane were in attendance. Dr. Deane gave the marquess a worried glance and shook his head.

"How are you, Giles?" Richard asked.

"My state of health should bring you pleasure, Richard," Giles answered derisively. He turned and asked those in attendance, "Would you mind if I had a private word with my brother?"

When they were alone, Richard asked, "What is it you wish to say?" His words were short and clipped.

Giles lay silent a moment, as if to gather strength.

"Richard, I want to make peace with you. I was wrong to take Lucinda, I never loved her. I only wanted to take revenge on you."

"Why, Giles, what did I ever do to merit your long years of hate?" Richard asked.

"You were born first. I should have been the Marquess of Marston and master of Marston Hall," Giles replied.

"Then you should have murdered me. It would have been better then the hell you put Lucinda through!" Richard answered.

"I'm not the only one who is to be faulted there. At least I gave her what she thought was love. You gave her nothing. She was too weak and missish for you. She was a woman who needed much attention and certainly coddling. Your guilt is as great as mine, for you never tried to give her the gentle treatment she needed."

Richard could not answer. The truth stabbed like a knife. "Why, Giles, did you?"

"I wanted her to have my son . . . who would inherit Marston Hall." Giles laughed with a chilling tinge of madness.

"My God, Giles, how could you? She killed herself over what she considered your abandonment."

"You purchased my colors and sent me away," Giles accused.

"Aye, and you never wrote her. You took a bride. That alone would have killed her," Richard countered.

"Yes, but you could have treated her with kindness," Giles said.

"I was never unkind. But I do not take the leavings of any man, not even my brother," Richard said, his anger beginning to show.

"Richard, I am going to die. I want to ask your forgiveness. I want to make peace with those around me before I—"

Richard thought of Katherine and his love for her. He bowed his head. He could almost understand. "But you never loved Lucinda," he stated.

"I did as much as I could love anyone," Giles replied.

"What of Katherine?" Richard asked with a flash of green fire in his eyes. The look did not go unnoticed by Giles.

"Why, dear brother, she was always for you. I brought her home for you to long for . . . thinking she was mine. And my noble brother would not stoop to the same depths of seduction as his brother had stooped. What a sweet revenge . . . but that is no longer important. I will not be here to see the torment in your eyes. Although I have already glimpsed it." He laughed with glittering eyes.

The image of Katherine came to Richard and a look of pain appeared in his eyes. Giles smiled. He did not know the depths of the wound he had inflicted, but he read the suffering on Richard's face.

"Giles, on one hand you ask forgiveness, and then on the other, you still are bent on my misery. Why?"

Giles was momentarily silent, his strength nearly all spent from the emotional exchange. "Take care of Katherine and Ellen, Richard. Not for me, but because they are innocent." He closed his eyes.

Richard waited a moment longer, but Giles did not speak again. He appeared to have fallen asleep, and his breathing was labored.

Crossing the room, the marquess called back the doctor and servants and left the hall to find solitude in his study.

Chapter 16

Giles died in his sleep. He slipped away silently and, at the very moment of his demise, unnoticed. It was after midnight and Katherine had retired. Norton had been sitting in attendance with his head resting back on the chair and his eyes closed. So the life given to envy and vengeance ebbed away with none to mourn his immediate passing.

Norton became aware that all was not right when he realized the room had become eerily silent. Sitting up in the chair, he glanced over to the prone patient. The realization that Giles was not breathing slowly crept over him. He rose and reached for Giles's hand, only to feel it had already turned cold.

Stunned, Norton stood, uncertain for a moment. Thinking of Miss Kate, he was unsure of which course to take. He decided to seek Lord Marston first.

Richard had just retired but was yet not asleep. His conversation with Giles had disturbed him immeasurably. He had long held his brother in disdain, rejecting Giles's callous treatment of the very people he owed care and concern. But Richard had not come away from their exchange unchanged. The high-toned disregard in which he had long held Giles now haunted his conscience, for he recognized how his brother's familial position had distorted his personality and led to his devious actions. He now felt sorry for Giles. Leading a life of demented envy must have been a private, eroding hell. Still, the wake of hurt Giles had left behind him could not be excused or easily forgiven.

Richard was a religious man and forgiveness was expected of him. Yet he had rejected Lucinda for her betrayal. It was what any man would do. Still, he had stood beside Lucinda by not divorcing her, and accepting Ellen. Richard shifted in discomfort for he knew he had not really accepted Ellen, only acknowledged her as his own.

Richard stretched his long frame and questioned if Lucinda would have taken her life had he made an attempt to show her compassion. He knew he had cared little one way or the other. His heart had been frozen in unforgiveness and indifference. True, Lucinda never expressed any regret. In fact, he could clearly remember her taunting reminder that Ellen was Giles's, not his.

He ran his hand through his thick hair and swore a silent oath. Damn. He could not change what was past, only attempt to create some semblance of order in his tangled emotions in the future.

He heard an impatient tap on his door and turned in surprise. Reaching for his dressing gown, Richard rose and was still tying his belt when he opened the door to see Norton's anxious face.

"My lord, forgive my interruption, but your brother—Lord Marston, your brother is dead," he blurted out.

"Fetch Dr. Deane," Richard ordered as he pushed past the giant of a man. "Has your mistress been informed?" he asked, pausing a moment.

"No, my lord, I sought you out first."

"Norton, summon Lady Amelia, inform her, and then instruct her to go to Katherine," he ordered.

He longed to go comfort her, but rejected that as totally unwise. His heart would lead him where he should not yet tread.

He was in Giles's bedchamber with the doctor when Katherine entered. She was pale and shaken, as was Lady Amelia, who trailed behind her. Richard crossed the room and took Kate's hand to express his condolences. Her hand felt slim and cold in his hand. His concerned eyes searched her face as she looked up at him.

"Richard, he knew he was going to die. He said . . ." She faltered and lowered her eyes.

A hard frown creased Lord Marston's face. Surely, he thought, he didn't tell her of Lucinda. I pray he did not, Lord, for she does not deserve that pain in addition to all she has suffered since coming into this family.

Katherine continued softly, "He said it would be a release."

Richard sighed in relief that Giles had shown at least a little discretion.

A profound sadness filled Katherine as she gazed at her dead husband. Her husband whom she had never really known. Her tears were of compassion for tormented Giles, not for her loss. She was honest enough to recognize that.

When she shifted her eyes to Richard, he was watching her intently and a wave of discomfort came over her. Quickly, she withdrew her hand.

Richard's eyes flickered and he turned away. How reluctant he was to let that slim hand slip from his grasp. He felt totally helpless.

Arrangements were made for the funeral with Giles's body laid out in state in the formal gold salon.

Katherine smiled ruefully as she donned the black bombazine dress she had ordered upon the insolent advice of the marquess so many weeks ago. Lady

Amelia was hovering over her like a mother hen, and Katherine was grateful. She moved as if in a nightmare. She felt overwhelmingly alone, and only the presence of Amelia was able to alleviate that feeling.

The Reverend Charles Whiteburn, Vicar of St. Mary's of the Lake, called early that morning. He greeted all the family members. "My dear Mrs. Swynford, my prayers are with you. Your husband's untimely death can only be remembered in the light of his brave service to his country," the thin bespectacled clergyman said.

Katherine nodded and thanked him for his kind words. She felt numb. She felt guilty that she could not mourn Giles. She felt only the desire to escape, to get away from Marston Hall and never return.

While she nodded at the vicar and smiled weakly, her eyes traveled over his thin shoulder to meet Richard's. He returned her look with a steady gaze, as if to say he understood.

Among the many carriages of friends and local gentry paying calls to the bereaved family, the carriage bearing Dr. Spencer arrived unnoticed as it pulled through the gates into the courtyard.

Katherine's father noted the black wreath and the crepe hung over the door. His blue eyes clouded with worry. I am too late for Giles, he thought. The carriage steps were let down and he quickly emerged to be greeted at the door by Latimer.

"I am Dr. Spencer, Mrs. Swynford's father," he said.

"Yes, Dr. Spencer. Come in. I am sad to inform you we are in mourning for Captain Swynford. Your daughter will welcome you," Latimer said in what was probably the longest and most intimate speech ever given to a stranger calling at Marston Hall. The crusty butler was a stickler for etiquette, but Katherine had long since won a place in his heart. He was very grateful for the arrival of the lady's own kin. He knew it would be a comfort to her.

He bowed and led the way to the gold saloon as Dr. Spencer had declined to change his clothes immediately, despite his long journey.

"Papa, oh Papa!" Kate cried just as Latimer was about to announce his arrival. She fairly flew across the room to him. No thought of the decorum of her actions entered her head. Throwing herself into his beloved arms, she shed the tears that had not come before now.

Richard approached the pair. "I am the Marquess of Marston, Richard Swynford, brother to Giles. I am grateful for your timely appearance. Allow me to show you to the library which will afford you and your daughter some private time."

Dr. Spencer appraised the young man before him as he shook his hand. He liked what he saw. Lord Marston was a man of strength and purpose, he thought.

"I decided to come upon receiving Katherine's last letter. I could discern Giles was failing. It appears I have preceded my letter announcing my intentions," he explained.

He put an arm around Kate's waist as they walked along the hall. "Kate, how do you fare?" he asked with all the concern a devoted father can bring. She did not immediately answer.

Richard seated them and offered some brandy to the doctor and took his leave. His eyes once more sought out Katherine, and he felt relief knowing her father was here for her.

"Oh, Father! It has not been what I expected," she cried when they were alone. "Of course, Giles has been so ill, but I've been so very lonely. I want to come home," she wailed, throwing her arms about him. Dr. Spencer held her tight and kissed her head.

"And so you shall, my love. But first we must see that your obligations are met." He fondly placed a comforting arm around her shoulder.

"Father, Giles told me before he died he . . . he never loved me. He just brought me to . . . to . . ." She could not finish her words. How could she explain Giles's strange behavior?

Dr. Spencer listened in patience to her fragmented account of the trials of her past few months. His heart sank. He had been somewhat reluctant to allow her marriage to the young Captain, and now that qualm had proven to be justified.

Knowing her infatuation with the handsome young man had come from her lack of exposure to other suitors, he acknowledged his own culpability. He had failed to recognize that she had grown into a beautiful woman who needed the love and companionship of a man. Therefore, she had been too vulnerable to the very considerable charms of Captain Swynford. How wrong he had been, for now she must pay the price of experience in a most unfortunate manner. Still, she was young and would recover, he told himself to ease his pain. But that thought gave him little comfort, for he himself had never recovered from the loss of his wife Margaret.

"Did you love him, Kate? Is the hurt beyond bearing, for I tell you time does dim the memory, if not the hurt," he sadly added, planting a kiss on her hair.

"Father, I do not know. I certainly thought so when I married him. He was so ill . . . the journey so long and hard. He would have lived, I know, if he had stayed in Dover. Father, he was never a husband, I mean he never . . . we never were man and wife. I thought it was only his illness, but he said he didn't love me," she cried once more. But of her feelings for Richard, she could not tell even her beloved father.

Sympathy flickered in the kind eyes of Dr. Spencer. He momentarily remembered the rich love that had existed between him and his wife. It was that happiness he had hoped his daughter could experience, but instead, she had found only heartache.

"Kate, you are young. You have many years yet to live. For now, we will deal with immediate problems. You will find that life has yet opportunities for happiness. I am here. Let us deal with the present and all will come to rights," he assured her.

When they returned to the gold salon, Katherine was surprised to see Cornelia Hampton had come to call. Clinging to Richard's arm, she was expressing her profound sorrow. Dr. Spencer felt his daughter stiffen beside him and he cast a curious look in the direction toward which she was gazing. He crooked an eyebrow in interest at the elegant lady.

Cornelia extended a hand to Katherine. "I am so saddened at your loss. Please accept my profound condolences. If I can be of any assistance, do not hesitate to call on me," she said with seeming sincerity.

"Thank you, Lady Hampton. May I present my father, Dr. Spencer," Katherine said in a dispirited voice.

"A pleasure, to be sure. It is so good that you are here. I suppose you will take Katherine back to Dover now. She would desire that above all, I'm sure." Lady Hampton smiled her aristocratic, patronizing smile.

"Yes, Lady Hampton, that is my intention," Dr. Spencer said, matching her coolness.

This time it was Richard who stiffened and frowned as he looked sharply at Katherine. Lady Hampton, whose hand was still on Richard's arm, felt his reaction. She turned questioningly to the marquess and did not like what she saw. Cornelia then turned and slid her eyes over Katherine's beautiful face, recognizing she had competition.

If Katherine was unaware of this exchange, the astute Dr. Spencer was not. So this is the way the wind blows, he thought.

Chapter 17

The mild autumn weather that had lingered through October, turned into black storms which filled the skies. Cold driving rain beat against the windows and great gusts of wind rattled the panes. Draperies billowed as the wind entered through cracks in the ancient house. A dark gloom settled in and the damp chill was difficult to ward off even with the fires lit in every grate.

Katherine stood by the window of the usually sunny breakfast room, watching the last few mums being beaten to the ground by the rain and wind. Watching the puddles form on the worn stones of the terrace, she pulled her cashmere shawl tight around her shoulders. Her gloom matched the pall that had settled over the household. Giles's funeral would take place in only a few hours. She shook her head in dejection. She felt numb, as if in limbo, and she chided herself for not feeling more. What kind of a woman was she, who felt nothing?

Pulling her shawl even tighter over her chest, she turned to see Amelia and her father entering the room.

"Good morning, Katherine. Were you able to sleep?" Amelia questioned, noting the dark circles under the young lady's eyes.

"Some," Katherine replied as she placed a kiss on the cheek of her aunt. Smelling the unmistakable lavender scent Amelia always wore, Katherine smiled faintly.

Dr. Spencer put a loving arm around his daughter's shoulder. "Kate, are you managing?" he asked, giving her a reassuring hug.

How could she tell him of her worry, her guilt over her lack of emotion toward Giles? She resented his having married her and bringing her to Marston Hall for devious reasons. She abhorred her attraction to Richard. It was all so wrong and against every principle in which she believed.

"My only wish is to survive this day, and return with you as soon as possible," she stated with a force that left little doubt of her desire to be gone from Marston Hall.

Richard entered the room in time to hear her last remark and a fierce frown crossed his handsome features. All three turned at Lord Marston's entrance. He was also dressed in mourning in an excellent cut coat of black superfine cloth. Dark rings showed beneath his eyes and strong line ran down one side of his set mouth. His eyes were worried.

"I know your stay here has been full of sorrow, Kate, but I hope we have made known how dear we hold you in our estimation. We wish only for your comfort and happiness," he said, feeling a pang of remorse as he remembered the exchange in the library that had probably set the seal on her desire to leave Marston. He could not fault her, only himself.

Katherine bit on her lower lip and felt her cheeks grow warm at the setdown to her ill-mannered remark. She cast Richard a scathing glance, remembering how he had called her an adventuress.

"My comment was not intended as a slight to the generous hospitality of your family. It only expressed a feeling that perhaps is best left unsaid," she countered with a stubborn rise of her chin. She returned his steady gaze and could not stop her response to those intense hazel-green eyes.

She turned to pick up a plate to choose from the many dishes on the sideboard. Richard felt a towering rage build inside him as he watched her. I'm going to lose her, he thought. She will simply leave, and I do not have the power to hold her. He stood a moment longer, then quickly left the room.

They all were surprised and taken aback but it was Amelia who exclaimed, "Why, whatever put him in the boughs?"

"I wonder," Dr. Spencer interjected as he took his place before the excellent breakfast set before him by a silent but very interested footman.

Sheets of rain continued to fall during the short trip to St. Mary's, turning roads to quagmires. Richard sat next to Katherine on the ride to the church but they did not speak. He carefully assisted her from the carriage and took her arm as they hurried up the steps and into the church. His umbrella did little to protect them, and they entered the building wet and chilled.

The only light in the church came from the flickering candles and the pale daylight that managed to enter through the stained-glass windows. Katherine could feel Richard's arm against hers as they sat close together in the family pew.

The Reverend Whiteburn droned on about the sacrifice of a fine example of manhood. Katherine kept her head lowered and her eyes hooded. She felt especially guilty for allowing her affection for Richard to grow and her feelings for Giles to die unattended.

Richard was equally conscious of Katherine's nearness, but he felt no guilt. He thoroughly understood what kind of a man Giles had been and believed he would somehow find a way to win Katherine. He knew that his *tendre* for Katherine, while by far too premature, was extremely strong. He took comfort in her nearness.

Following the funeral service, the mourners moved

out to the gravesite, where a large canopy had been erected over the final resting place in the small graveyard that held the Swynford ancestors. The rain continued unabated and the voice of the Reverend Whiteburn was almost drowned out by the pelting rain on the canvas. The damp chill penetrated the marrow of everyone gathered there. It was a rather fitting end to Giles's life, Richard mused. He did, however, feel sorry that Giles had been unable to find or give so little happiness. Richard's greatest regret was that he had allowed Giles to color his own life with cynicism. And that cynicism had caused him to hurt Kate.

At last, the ordeal was over and the family returned in subdued spirits to the shelter of Marston Hall.

Cook had prepared a hearty country luncheon to ward off the chill and dampness. A rich beef and barley soup was followed by roast mutton, creamed turnips, and a charlotte russe. A rich port was served and gave a sense of sated security to the weary family members. The warmth even invaded Katherine's icy veins.

As was customary, solicitors arrived later that afternoon to read the last will and testament of Captain Swynford. It was a duty that had to be performed, though Richard wished to put it off. Closeted in his study with the two barristers who had handled the affairs of the Swynfords for years, Richard exacted a pledge from the astonished lawyer that one provision not be read aloud at this time.

"Highly irregular," pronounced one Mr. Roberts as the other nodded in agreement.

"I do not give a damn. It is not to be read. The young widow is not to be troubled with such details at this most bereaved moment. Do you understand?" Richard demanded.

"Of course, your lordship, it shall be as you wish,"

the thin barrister replied as his brother nodded in agreement.

Richard realized his request would raise questions about the reason for the provision. But he did not care. He would risk speculation to protect Katherine.

Amelia, Richard, and Katherine were called to be present as was expected. One Mr. Roberts adjusted his spectacles and the other cleared his throat and began to read. They're like two dried-up peas in a pod, Amelia thought, watching the thin solicitors begin the proceedings.

Katherine was left Merrywood and the use of its income during her lifetime. All monies were bequeathed to Katherine. Certain pieces of jewelry were given to Amelia and Ellen with the remainder left to Katherine. These, of course, were family pieces and were dispersed accordingly. There were legacies to certain servants and monies to be given the church.

Since Katherine had never inherited anything, she failed to note it odd that she was given Merrywood only for her lifetime. Amelia was amazed at this provision and raised her eyes to Richard's stony, implacable face. His lips were drawn in a fine white line. Confused, she lowered her eyes again. Why had there been no mention of the person to whom the estate would pass upon Katherine's death? She would let it rest, for now, but vowed to put the question to Richard at a more opportune time.

The household returned to a more normal routine within a few days. Katherine found she had endless time on her hands, since she no longer had Giles to look after. She spent many delightful hours with Ellen since she was now very attached to the little girl.

Her spirits began to rise and her laughter was heard more and more often as the camaraderie between

Katherine and her father returned. It was so good to be with him once more, she thought.

The staff was pleased, for Katherine had endeared herself to them all. They had seen her devotion to Captain Swynford. They had felt her kindness and appreciation for the services rendered on her behalf. So Katherine had a devoted following among the servants at Marston Hall.

It amused Richard to know that the servants obeyed him out of respect but Kate out of love. His orders had been subtly overridden more than once by a servant telling him that Mrs. Swynford would wish this or that. He always deferred to Katherine with a twinkle of amusement. So she reigned supreme in the servants' quarters.

The weather continued to be abominable, which made any excursion impossible. Of course, outings were very limited because of the period of mourning, but a carriage ride would have been welcome.

Katherine constantly made references to her return to Dover. These remarks were met with stony silence by Richard and a disappointed expression from Amelia.

During dinner, one evening, Katherine again mentioned her desire to return home. "Father, when do you expect we shall return to Dover? I should imagine you are anxious to return to your work."

"I thought you would want to spend Christmas with Ellen. We could plan to leave the first of the year. How does that strike you?" he asked.

"Christmas! Father, that's more than six weeks away. How can you be gone so long?" she asked in utter surprise.

"You are aware that my new assistant is quite capable," he answered.

"I, too, intend to leave at the first of the year," interjected Lady Amelia. "I plan to return to Bath after the winter holidays. I came, as you know, to be with Richard and Ellen in their time of need. My stay was, of

course, extended because of Giles. But I shall no longer
be needed. My, my, Richard, your household will certainly be reduced. How will you manage with Ellen
alone?" She watched Katherine very carefully as she
made her remarks.

"We'll manage," he tersely replied.

Katherine felt a quick tightening in her chest at the
thought of Ellen left alone in this huge house with only
Richard and the servants. Poor Ellen, she thought, and
turned her eyes to her plate.

"I fear Ellen will sorely miss you, Katherine. Far too
much, to be sure. Have you ever considered taking up
residence at Merrywood? Then Ellen would not be
deprived of your love and concern, which she has come
to depend upon," Amelia said, seeming all innocence.

Katherine slowly lowered her spoon. She looked
totally surprised. "No, I have never considered it . . ."

"Katherine, you could be happy at Merrywood. You
said you loved the house when we visited it. Ellen could
accompany you, if you wished. I would promise to see
her often," Richard suggested with a watchful expression.

"Impossible! I must return to Dover," she said.

Paul Spencer looked at his daughter's determined expression and knew she would not change her decision.
He adored her and found much pleasure in her
company, so much so that he had previously kept her
too sheltered from male companionship. But now he
knew she was no longer his little protected daughter.
She had grown up. She must now seek her own destiny,
and like any father he now wondered about the correct-
ness of her decision. He looked at Lord Swynford and
felt the extraordinary effort the marquess was exerting
to control his cool features.

Dr. Spencer had an opportunity, that evening, to test
his theory, when he found himself alone with Richard
after the ladies had retired.

"Dr. Spencer, do you think it possible for me to convince Katherine to remain at Merrywood?"

"Not if she is determined to go."

"I see. Are you as determined to take her to Dover?"

"I am only committed to my daughter's happiness."

"Yes, so am I. Her happiness is most important to me. Her destiny is here with me. I love Katherine," Richard said as he shrugged in a rather helpless manner.

"You do not surprise me with your declaration."

"That transparent, eh?"

"No, but I have seen you look at her. I also think it is up to you to change her mind."

"Well, yes, of course. But I do not know how to go about it. I have made grave errors where she is concerned. It is so soon after Giles's death and I would not want to offend her. I do not know her feelings. I suspect she does not think well of me. And she has every right, to be sure!" Richard said, looking woebegone.

"I suppose all that is true; still, Giles told Katherine before he died that he never loved her. He asked her for forgiveness. That makes the circumstances different, I should think," Paul Spencer explained, hoping against hope he had not betrayed his daughter's confidence.

"Damn, but Giles was a fool. Did it hurt her?"

"I don't think so. I don't really know. There never really was an opportunity for a lasting sort of affection to grow between them. If Giles did not love her . . . it is beyond my ken why he married her. Kate was surely infatuated with him in the beginning, at least. But I can tell you, I do not like what has been done. And so I will gladly take her home, if that is what will make her happy," he said with determination.

"Dr. Spencer, I should like to explain to you about Giles. You must promise not to tell Katherine. I would not have her hurt anymore. If I am to succeed in pressing my suit . . . it must be for me that she accepts.

Not because of what Giles did or her love of Ellen. It must be me she wants.''

Paul Spencer liked what he heard. He was a good judge of men and had come to respect the gentleman who sat before him. He would suit Katherine well, he thought.

Richard began to speak. He did not color any details or gloss over any facts. As he spoke steadily, he felt a growing relief, for it felt good to lay bare the wounds of the past few years. He did not, however, describe the night he had held Kate in his arms in this very room. That wonderful moment which he carried close to his heart, belonged to no one else but Katherine and himself.

By the time Richard finished his story, the fire was nothing but embers softly glowing in the hearth and the brandy glasses were empty. Paul Spencer rose to retire. ''My lord, you have my blessings to woo Katherine. I shall not aid or abet you—the decision will be hers, alone—however, I truly believe you would suit one another.''

''Thank you, Dr. Spencer.''

''Paul, please. If we are to be—well, let it be Paul. Please.''

''Yes, Paul. Thank you once more.''

The two men who loved Katherine parted on the best of terms.

ter 18

Chapter 18

Katherine stretched her body languorously. The cozy warmth and comfort of her bed with its linens that smelled faintly of lavender enticed her to linger longer. Sleep still clung to the edges of her mind and she gave in to the luxurious feeling, by snuggling deeper among the covers.

She had been awakened by a maid quietly adding wood to the fire. The young maid begged Katherine's pardon at her intrusion as she dropped her a curtsy, explaining that a winter chill was in the air, then quickly left the room. The embers sprang into crackling flames, adding to the sense of well-being Katherine was experiencing.

Several days had passed since Giles's funeral and Kate thought with surprise and pleasure that today she was more herself. She smiled at the thought. It would be wonderful to feel happy again. And she realized that was exactly how she now felt.

A frown creased her forehead and she wondered, once more, if she were a heartless woman. Her husband lay dead and buried less than a week and here she was snuggled among the covers feeling almost euphoric. Katherine had avoided thinking of Giles, for she could not do so without feeling overwhelming guilt. She examined the idea for a moment. He had said he had not loved her when he begged her forgiveness for bringing her to Marston. At his bedside she had consented to do just that, but she had not really forgiven him in her heart. She was still too hurt by his rejection. If he didn't love her, why had he wooed her with such vigor? Why had he married her?

Without invitation, the image of Richard entered her mind. She felt a rush of warmth spread through her body. She was attracted to him, no doubt. But was it more than attraction? Did she love him? She threw her arm over her eyes to send the image away.

She almost could feel his presence, see his intense eyes that watched her like a panther does his prey. A chill tingled through her body as she remembered how those hazel-green eyes flashed fire and, on other occasions, softened with a question. She knew she rebuffed his every glance.

Suddenly, Katherine's sense of well-being began to fade, and doubt seized her once more. She held no illusions about Richard's opinion of her. He had made that clear the night he had held her in his arms and kissed her. Adventuress! Indeed, he is an arrogant fool, she thought, and I shall not succumb to his considerable charms again.

She smiled wryly, thinking that the Swynford men certainly had charm. She decided she would not make that mistake again. Her headlong rush to wed Giles had brought only regret. She recognized Richard was twice as dangerous, for he aroused her feelings much more than Giles ever had. Her body was traitor to her where Richard was concerned.

Despite her vows, she still deeply longed to be held and loved by Richard. Well, I shall not be foolish, she decided firmly. I will be more than vigilant where he is concerned and avoid him like the plague. Kate decided to press her father to leave Marston immediately.

She rolled over and buried her head in the pillow. She would not make that demand and she knew it. Heavens, how ambivalent she was. Why, she wondered? Her mind latched onto Ellen, and she rationalized that Ellen needed her like a mother. The child needed love and attention. Richard certainly wouldn't give Ellen any, and it wasn't right to leave the little girl alone with him.

Thoroughly exasperated with herself, Katherine threw back the covers and swung her legs over the edge of the bed. The chill hit her like a slap as she grabbed for her heavy velvet robe. Her thoughts were like a weather vane, first turning one way, then another. She needed time, she reasoned, to sort them all out.

It was late morning and Katherine turned Ellen over to Nanny Burke to feed and put to bed for her afternoon nap.

"His lordship is in the antechamber and requests to see you," Nanny Burke whispered as she took the child from Kate's arms.

A soft flush spread over Katherine's cheeks and she smoothed her hair. "Whatever for?" she asked.

"Didn't say, Mrs. Swynford," Nanny answered, turning her attention to Ellen and carrying her off to her waiting noontime meal.

Katherine entered the small room to find Lord Marston standing with one foot on a window seat and a riding crop in his hand. He was dressed in buckskin riding breeches and coat which fitted perfectly and accented his exceedingly masculine body. He straightened up at her entrance.

"Yes, your lordship, what do you wish to see me about?" she asked with a decided chill to her voice.

He watched her cross the room, thinking that even in mourning attire, she was gorgeous. Her black woolen gown accented her dark hair and made her blue eyes striking. She stopped and raised her face to his in question. He wanted to reach out and touch her.

"Katherine, I have sought you out because you avoid

me at every turn," he said, his rich voice quietly lowered.

"Do I?" she asked with a slight shrug.

"You know you do and I want to find out why," he replied with a gleam of amusement. It was not like her to play coy.

Katherine's eyes hardened and she returned his look with a steady stare. "I think you can answer that one, my lord."

Richard shifted uncomfortably. "Aye, and I am here to beg your forgiveness. It was improper, and rude of me and you did not deserve such treatment. I can only plead human frailty, and vow never to foist myself upon you again. I was exceedingly wrong. This is my house and under its roof you will have full protection. I shall never overstep that boundary again. Can you forgive me? May we make a truce?"

She was silent for a moment. "It seems that the Swynford men are forever in need of my forgiveness," she said ungraciously.

"That may be true but it is unfair. Now it is you who are rude." His voice was edged with anger.

"Yes, well, if you will forgive me, then I shall forgive you and we will make a truce," she said contritely, a little embarrassed by her rudeness.

"Good." He held his hand out in a gesture of agreement, his eyes twinkling with pleasure.

This irked her, for she did not wish him to think that he could so easily manipulate her.

"There is one thing, my lord. You did call me an adventuress and I sorely resent it," she retorted.

"Oh, Kate, do not remind me of that. It would be a burden I could not bear, if you would not forget and forgive me that." The sadness and sincerity in his voice sent a pang through Katherine's heart. He reached up and took her chin in his hand and his thumb traced her jawline. "You were never anything but courageous, and could I but take back those words . . ."

She was captured by his touch as well as his words.

They stood a moment longer while Richard resisted the desire to bring his lips to hers.

"We will have your truce, then, Richard."

He smiled, a smile that reached his eyes. Her heart surged.

Richard let his hand drop. "Thank you, Kate. One more thing—do consider the advantages of Merrywood for yourself and Ellen. It would make me infinitely happy," he whispered.

"But will it do the same for me?"

He paused. "That, only you can answer, but it is my belief that it would be the best choice." He turned and moved to the door. "Thank you, Kate." Then he was gone. The room suddenly seemed dark, as if the sun had moved behind a cloud.

Katherine stood unmoving for several moments. She needed to discuss this with her father and perhaps Amelia.

Dr. Spencer was delighting himself among the stacks of the extensive library when Kate found him. "Good afternoon, child," he said as she entered the room.

"Father, I wish to speak to you. Richard has spoken with me to make amends. He has been hateful, you know!"

"No, I did not," he replied with amusement. "Come sit next to me. Now, that's better. What is it you wish to speak of?" He struggled to match the serious expression on Kate's face. But he was finding it difficult since he more than enjoyed observing Richard's tactics.

"Richard feels I should seriously consider taking up residence at Merrywood. He thinks Ellen needs me. What do you think?" she asked, shifting on the settee.

Paul Spencer smiled and reached for his daughter's

hand. "Kate, it is for you to decide. But the decision does not have to be made immediately, for our departure is not for more than a month. Use the time to make up your mind. I do not want to sway you in any direction, but Merrywood is yours, and it seems to me there is a strong bond between you and Ellen." He answered with gravity, for he knew the decision would not be easy. He would watch with interest as Richard wooed Kate. He would be delighted if Richard's courtship became the reason she chose to stay.

Luncheon was served shortly after Katherine's conversation with her father. The atmosphere was congenial, with Richard discussing the merits of country living.

He's doing it up a bit brown, thought Dr. Spencer as he listened to Richard's monologue on the vast appeal of life in the country.

"That is well enough for you, Richard, but I should very much miss society with its many diversions," Lady Amelia countered.

"Now, Amelia, do not say that! I have just this morning tried to convince Katherine to remain at Merrywood and am trying to convince her of the charming aspects of a bucolic existence," Richard good-naturedly chided his aunt.

Lady Amelia looked up at Richard and smiled. "Indeed? Well, that is a different matter entirely. I shall then extol the virtues of Merrywood and the beauty of its land. Managing an estate would be a marvelous challenge, much more engrossing than some silly routs and balls." She laughed, winking at Katherine. "Of course, it must be Katherine's decision. I would not for the world try to influence her."

Katherine laughed and sat back in her chair. "That is the third time today I have been told how advantageous it would be for me to remain, but of course none of my advisers wish to influence me. Since, of course, it is *my* decision. I am beginning to think you are all in conspiracy," she teased.

"You wrongly accuse us. We are just very intelligent persons who love you and wish for your happiness." Amelia chuckled and looked to Richard for confirmation.

"Aye, she is correct, you know. Three finer minds you could not find to 'not influence you.' And if Ellen spoke her heart, I'm sure she would agree with us," he teased.

Paul Spencer smiled. " 'Tis your wishes, though, Kate, that must be met."

"So I've been told, but somehow I feel outnumbered," she said, raising her hands in mock surrender. "Still, the idea of being mistress of my own domain is attractive. The prospect of being chatelaine of my own castle, as it were, is not without charm," she replied with a twinkle.

Richard sat back in his chair with a rush of relief. He had observed the exchange with intense control, not wishing to show his decided interest in her reply. He had not wanted to put her on the defensive.

He was amazed at the ease with which the conversation had transpired. He had expected to have to mount a battle to make her recant her decision to leave. It had been easy, too easy. He did not quite trust her capitulation. He held his breath, and his heart raced in fear he would hear otherwise.

"Ellen will be secure with you. I feared for her. No offense, Richard. It's just that the child has lost her mother and Katherine has been more the mother than her own ever was. You will have to forgive my predilection for plain truth," Amelia said with a slight determined rise of her chin.

"None taken, Amelia. I am equally grateful for Katherine's decision," he said with a placid expression that belied his inner turmoil.

Katherine was amazed at how easy it had been to make her decision to stay. She had never intended to do so. Still, here she had just made that choice and a feeling of eagerness and anticipation filled her.

"Richard, may I speak with you a moment," she asked when she rose from the table. She had decided to use this opportunity to talk to him about Ellen.

Lord Marston looked up in surprise and rose at her request. He was still apprehensive about her ready decision to remain and was eager to hear whatever it was she wished to say. "Shall we move to the library?" he said, taking her by the arm. Katherine wanted to distance herself from him, but rather than make an obvious gesture of pulling away, she allowed him to escort her into the library. Her heart beat too quickly at his touch and she forced herself to wear a detached expression.

Upon entering the handsome room, she quickly moved to a chair set somewhat apart and sat down. Richard remained standing and watched the serious expression on her face.

"What is it, Katherine?" he asked, crossing his arms across his chest and gazing down at her with keen interest.

"Sit down, Richard, I can't talk to you while you stand over me like some schoolmaster!" she said.

He smiled and obeyed, pulling up a chair to be nearer her.

"I wish to speak of Ellen. Since I am to remain for her welfare, I must tell you that I feel your behavior to her is sorely lacking. It is most unnatural for a father, and I know she feels your absence of love," she said in all sincerity and utter bluntness.

Richard sat back and watched her a moment. She was correct and he knew it, but it had never mattered. Ellen had always been Giles's. He could not tell her that, or at least he did not wish to. He had deliberately used her growing love for the child as a ploy to hold her at Merrywood. He had used the child as a pawn, which was dishonorable. He frowned and searched a moment for the right words.

"My marriage was unhappy, Katherine, and I fear that led to my indifference for the child. She loves and needs you. That is why I have asked you to care for her at Merrywood," he answered in a reasonable-sounding untruth. His eyes clouded at his manipulative words, but he knew he must keep Katherine near at any cost. He quickly quelled any guilt. "Would you remain at Marston Manor?" he asked.

"No, Richard, you know I would not. I'll stay for Ellen, but I must have my own home," she said with an equal half truth. "She must have the opportunity to know you. She needs her father," Katherine insisted.

A muscle twitched in Richard's jaw and he twisted his signet ring in an uneasy manner. "Kate, you are, of course, correct. I will truly make the effort to know my . . . Ellen. She needs you but I vow to spend more time and attention on her. Will that suit you for now?" he quietly asked.

Katherine felt a profound sadness in his voice and wondered at it. "Do you think you can come to care for her?" she asked.

A pain stabbed at his heart and he placed his hand over her clenched fist. "Kate, I will not disappoint you. But give me time to know . . . my daughter," he said hesitantly.

Katherine saw the pain in his eyes and nodded. "I will hold you to that promise, for you are her parent, not I, and you must take that responsibility."

"Aye, and I shall," he replied.

Katherine accepted this as the best she could achieve for now. She did not doubt for one moment that Ellen would soon have her father enchanted and her own presence would no longer be needed. She dismissed that thought immediately. Time will tell, she thought as she rose and left Richard sitting in the library.

Richard sighed a great sigh of relief. He had won. Now he must win Katherine.

Chapter 19

Once the decision was made, Katherine became less apprehensive about her future. She was still plagued by memories of her marriage, her guilt over her betrayal of Giles, and her feelings toward Richard. Richard could still send her heart racing whenever he entered the room. He could dominate a room just by his presence. Often he would stop to speak to her and the look in his eyes would send her reeling. Though she was able to hide these emotions rather well, she was always acutely conscious of him whenever he was near.

As the days passed, her sense of humor returned and a buoyancy appeared in her manner. Laughter and running footsteps again echoed through the manor's halls. Richard, likewise, suddenly seemed more content and began to show flashes of humor Katherine had never seen before. His harsh, guarded demeanor seemed to melt before her eyes. She was witnessing a side of Richard she had never known before and found it infinitely appealing.

Richard still kept a distance between them, but he was less restrained. He often joined Katherine and Ellen in the nursery or for an outing on days when the weather permitted. Her heart would leap when she saw him approach, or turned to find his eyes upon her. Katherine was always aware of his presence and dreams of him haunted her nights.

She noted he never attempted to seek her out while she was alone, but was gratified with his new interest in Ellen and told him so one morning after his visit to the nursery.

"Richard, thank you for spending time with Ellen. She is delighted with your attention and asks for you often. Is that not so, Nanny Burke?" Katherine turned to the nurse for confirmation.

"Aye, my lord, she profits mightily from your visits," Nanny Burke answered as she picked the child up to carry her into the child's sleeping chamber for nap time.

Richard smiled at the both of them and turned to escort Katherine to the dining room for luncheon. He took her arm and led her from the nursery. He did not have the heart to tell Katherine he used Ellen as an excuse to be with her. However, in all honesty, he was becoming more interested in the child.

"It is true, Richard. The child adores you," Katherine said as she lifted her eyes to him.

The question that Katherine had seen so often in his eyes appeared again. He paused a moment before starting down the steps and placed his hand over hers.

"Do not think I need to be complimented for my parental concern. Circumstances were different in the past, but they have changed. I am equally enchanted with the child. It's just that . . . well, no mind. It's a pleasure to get to know my daughter," he said.

As they descended the staircase, Lady Hampton crossed the hall to greet them. She was stunning in a sapphire velvet gown of the latest *beau monde* fashion, and the effect of the color on her red-gold curls and pale blue eyes was marvelous. She flashed a most beguiling smile. "Lady Amelia has requested that I stay for luncheon. I simply could not refuse, for it is such a pleasure to spend time here at Marston. I find the company vastly interesting." She simpered.

As they reached the bottom of the staircase, Lady Hampton reached out and placed her hand on Richard's other arm. He tightened his hold on Katherine's hand when he felt her begin to remove it.

"Of course. We have so much charm, I'm considering exporting it," Richard remarked dryly.

Lady Hampton trilled with laughter as she fell into step on his other side. "La, Richard, I do believe you could become vastly wealthy in doing so," she said flirtatiously, her eyes seeking his.

Good Heavens, Katherine thought in annoyance, every time I turn around, it seems I'm tripping over the overanxious, overripe, and overwilling widow. "Why, I believe we must count you as one of Marston Hall's many charms, Lady Hampton. You are here so often, it almost seems you are a part of the manor." Kate's words slipped out before she could stop them.

Once more, Lady Hampton trilled with laughter. The sound sent a grating shiver down Katherine's spine.

"My, Mrs. Swynford, you flatter me!"

Katherine felt Richard's arm tighten at this sally, and when she looked up at him, he was unsuccessfully smothering a smile. She beamed inwardly with satisfaction at her small success.

A slight frown, however, appeared on Katherine's face as she was assisted to her place by a footman.

Paul Spencer watched his daughter and smiled at the annoyed look on her face. Perhaps Richard was not as obtuse about the way to win a woman as he had seemed. Jealousy was certainly a good weapon to use to win a lady's heart. Yet he wondered if Katherine was not jealous but, like himself, simply tired of the overwilling Lady Hampton, whose whole conversation centered around herself. He steeled himself for another boring table conversation. He looked at Katherine and rolled his eyes.

Katherine giggled. If only I had had the foresight to

have a megrim, she thought. Since Lady Hampton seldom gave warning of her arrival, that would have been difficult. She just appeared whenever she chose, as if her visits were epiphanies, and all would be delighted at her arrival.

Raising an eyebrow, Richard turned sharply at the sound of Katherine's laugh. He smiled at her innocent expression.

Fortunately, Amelia carried the conversation with Lady Hampton during luncheon. Well aware of the tension caused by the guest, Amelia assumed her best society manners and joined in the wearisome topic of the latest London gossip.

"Father, do ride with me to Merrywood this afternoon. I should like very much to tour it again. Perhaps there are changes I might wish to make before I take up residence," Katherine remarked during a small lull in the conversation.

"It will be my pleasure. Time hangs heavy for me. I am not used to such idleness," he answered.

"Yes, that is what worries me about remaining at Merrywood. But perhaps I will be able to learn to take an active part in the running of the estate." Katherine sighed.

"Believe me, Katherine, if you do, you will find there is never enough time," Richard encouraged.

"Merrywood!" exclaimed Lady Hampton. "Why, Mrs. Swynford, are you planning to remain here?" Her face plainly showed her displeasure at such an idea. She had planned to carry on her siege of Richard without interference from Giles's beautiful widow. She had long noted that Richard looked constantly to the young woman. Her heart sank at such a prospect. "Surely you will be utterly bored in the country!" she warned.

Katherine smiled her sweetest smile. "Highly unlikely, for I have never partaken of London society and think it would hardly suit. I shall have time to spend with Ellen and that is my greatest wish."

"Well, of course, she is a dear. But she has her nurse, and that should be quite sufficient," Lady Hampton continued.

"The decision has been made. Father, are you ready?" Katherine asked as she rose from the table. This woman was too much, Katherine thought. She cast Richard a sideways glance and found him watching her with an encouraging smile. She returned it, much to the dismay of the elegant Lady Hampton, who could hear the death knell of her plans.

The days that followed passed in pleasant monotony until the excitement of Christmas began to fill the residents of Marston Hall. Dr. Spencer had made arrangements to return to Dover after Katherine's removal to Merrywood. Amelia decided she would spend a week helping Katherine to settle in, then return to her own home.

The hall was decorated with greens and mistletoe. The wonderful aromas of the plum and brandy cakes that would grace the holiday tables emanated from the kitchen.

Katherine spent an exorbitant amount of time finding a gift for Richard. Though Amelia did not question this effort, she was amused by it. On several occasions, she and Katherine, dressed warmly in their pilgrim coats to ward off the winter's chill, had gone to Alnwick to tramp through the stores of the local merchants in search of what Katherine deemed "just the right thing."

In a curio shop, Katherine finally found an exquisite carved ivory diptych. It was of Roman origin and she was amazed to find such a treasure in the small cluttered shop.

"How came you by this?" she asked the ancient proprietor.

"I have had this in my possession for many years. You are the first to show much interest in it. I obtained it from a noble lady that, eh, needed funds," he explained.

"I should like to purchase it. What is the price?" she asked.

He hesitated. "I am deeply attached to it, and I am not convinced I should sell it," he replied cagily, for he could see the lady was very interested and might pay well for the piece. Katherine turned to Amelia in confusion.

"My good man, do not foist your cheating ways on us. Either it is or it is not for sale. Name your price!" Amelia's helpless fluttering ways had disappeared. Katherine, delighted at the transformation, let a laugh escape her lips.

The wizened man thought her levity meant perhaps her desire to purchase the diptych was not so great after all, and he named a price.

"Outrageous!" Amelia snapped. "Katherine, I am convinced we can find something equally appealing for Lord Marston elsewhere."

"Lord Marston? Well, in that case I shall give you a better price," he hastily replied, for the marquess was his landlord.

The price was settled, and the purchase was made. Katherine teased Amelia all the way home to Marston about her formidable bargaining powers.

Amelia snorted. "Bargaining is no different from catching a man, Katherine. You just don't show your hand too quickly."

Katherine went into gales of laughter as they entered the hall. The happy sound echoed through the manor. Richard emerged from his study to find the cause of such merriment. He used any excuse he could to be with the woman who was always on his mind.

"You must share the reason for such laughter," he demanded, smiling himself, for her merriment was contagious.

"Why, Amelia has just informed me how to catch a man!" She smiled over at Amelia.

The elderly lady only frowned. "Katherine, one never reveals one's tactics. My goodness, you must keep that sort of thing to yourself," she teased.

"You're looking to catch a man?" Richard joined in, his eyes glittering.

Katherine stopped laughing and looked sharply at Richard. "Heavens no, why would I want a husband?" she replied, her eyes dancing.

Richard's smile faded. A glint entered his eyes. "Yes, why indeed would you want a husband?" He was no longer amused.

Amelia followed Katherine up the stairs and when they reached her door she turned and said, "You learn well, Katherine."

"What do you mean?"

"Why just now, the way you handled Richard, not showing your hand too soon," Amelia teased.

"Amelia! I do not set my cap for Richard!" Katherine protested.

"My dear, you cannot cozen me any more than the proprietor could," the elderly lady said with a knowing smile.

"Amelia, where did you get such an idea?" Katherine asked, her heart beating rapidly and a flush rising to her cheeks.

Amelia realized her remark had disturberd rather than amused Katherine and she backed down immediately.

"Forgive an old lady's overvivid imagination, my

dear. It's just that I think you are both ideally suited. I will say no more," she said in regret.

Katherine stood a moment, not knowing what to say. "Richard has a very low opinion of me. He has said as much."

"Indeed, then it is not I who am cozening you; you are cozening yourself," Amelia added, and she leaned over and kissed Katherine on her cheek. "He doesn't take his eyes off you," she added as a parting remark.

Watching the retreating figure of the diminutive lady, Katherine smiled and hoped that was so.

Chapter 20

Christmas Day was clear and crisp. The ground was covered with only a scattering of snow, which sparkled like diamonds in the sun. Silvery fingers of frost splayed out over the windows in feathery designs.

The marquess stretched his long frame, lingering in bed before rising to begin the day. He hoped it would prove happy. Thinking of Katherine, he wondered if her feelings of resentment toward him were fading. He sighed, thinking how wrong he had been. She was warm and loving, putting the cares of those she loved above all else, and he cringed to remember his accusations to her.

He had classified and judged her prematurely because of her beauty. Why had he assumed beauty meant selfishness? Had Lucinda colored his thoughts so much he had foolishly considered all beautiful women vain and shallow? Such jaded thinking had rendered his judgment so faulty he had probably lost any chance with the only woman he had truly wanted.

Wincing at the memory of his treatment of her the first night he had met her, he despaired of making amends. He remembered the night he had held her and kissed her. God, how he had wanted her. He would have taken her, and she had come willingly into his arms. The image sent a warmth through his body and he ached for her. But while she had not been indifferent to him, his lovemaking had probably ruined any chance he had of winning her. How could he overcome the past? Despair filled him.

She had said she would forgive him and of late their relationship was certainly of a more amiable nature. Still, there was that vague sense of strain between them. He would listen to her footsteps in the hall and anxiously await her arrival in a room, only to feel a distance spring between them as soon as she appeared. Skillfully, she avoided him. How could he fault her for that? He could not.

He knew the impropriety of wooing his brother's widow so soon after his death, so he refrained from making any overt move. Yet the need, the desire, and the pain of seeing her daily left him more and more anxious. Though he prided himself on being a man of controlled emotions, he recognized just how brittle and thin his veneer now was. He would eventually overstep the line of propriety. It was just a matter of time. Would she hate him? Would she reject him? That thought lowered his spirits even further.

Richard threw back his covers as Robbins entered the room. Dejected, he vowed he would keep a close guard on his actions. He could not lose any slight chance he had to win her.

Robbins, seeing the scowl on his lordship's face, quietly busied himself preparing his master's clothes.

When at last Richard entered the breakfast room, he looked handsome in his black coat and pantaloons. His collar, while not proclaiming him a Corinthian, was in the latest fashion and Robbins had managed to make an elegant waterfall in his snowy white neckcloth. A ruby sparkled in the folds.

The family had assembled for the morning meal and everyone greeted Richard with holiday wishes. Richard surveyed the little gathering, his eyes lingering on Katherine. Holding in his feelings, he nodded a rather curt good morning. His demeanor sent a chill through the room and its occupants.

"Richard, what has set you off? You look as black as the devil's heart!" Amelia said, taking him to task. " 'Tis Christmas and you look as if you've lost your last friend. Do not cast a pall over us with your dark looks."

Richard turned and smiled. "You are absolutely correct. It is Christmas and we shall celebrate the season as well as we can," he said lightly as he took his place at the head of the table.

Katherine watched him with dismay. Dressed in a new black water-silk gown trimmed with lace and with her hair in a rather elaborate Grecian arrangement in honor of the holiday, she was resisting a melancholy spirit herself. She had even taken the liberty of placing a sprig of holly on her dress in a small effort to lift her spirits.

The family attended Christmas services at St. Mary's. The ride through the sparkling countryside in the brisk air seemed to infuse the party with a more festive attitude. Ellen fidgeted and whispered the entire service, much to the annoyance of Reverend Whiteburn, who had spent a great deal of time preparing his far too lengthy sermon. Richard seemed totally unperturbed by the child's wiggles and giggles and Katherine smiled up at him under her poke bonnet. Richard met her eyes a moment with amusement in his own, then turned back to the droning service.

After church services, the family returned to Marston Hall and assembled in the salon, which had been decorated with fresh greens, holly, and mistletoe. A huge yule log was lit and sent a cheerful glow throughout the room.

Ellen, dressed in white velvet trimmed with lace and ribbons, was brought in to share the gift giving. Her eyes danced with anticipation as she surveyed the special candies and cookies the cook had prepared for the holiday. She reached shyly for the fairy princess doll her father presented her and hugged it tightly, declaring, "She's pretty, just like Aunt Katherine!" Everyone laughed. Spirits soared as they enjoyed the little girl and her excitement at so many gifts. It was not long before Nanny Burke carried the sleepy child from the room before the other gifts were distributed.

Katherine tensed as she watched Richard open her present to him. At first he was astounded, and quickly looked over to her. "Where did you find such a magnificent gift?" he asked.

"Believe it or not, right in Alnwick. Amelia helped me acquire it. I know you are partial to ancient works. I do hope you will enjoy owning it," she said with a slight breathlessness and flush in her cheeks. Katherine was truly gratified for she could see he was fascinated by the small ivory carving by the way his slender fingers caressed its delicate beauty.

"I believe it depicts Psyche and Eros." He smiled and raised his eyes to her. Crooking an eyebrow, he said, "And as you remember, she did not trust him enough to abide by his wishes."

Katherine held Richard's eyes a moment before dropping her gaze. Richard said softly, "It pleases me, beyond measure. It is a treasure and I appreciate it. Thank you." Picking up two packages, he handed them to Katherine.

Katherine took the gifts from Richard and opened the first package. It contained a beautiful pair of earrings made of sapphires surrounded by diamonds.

"Richard, they are stunning!" she exclaimed, carefully lifting the sparkling jewels in her hand.

"They will match your eyes. No other woman could wear them as well," he added quietly.

Katherine laughed at the compliment and her appreciation was obvious. The next gift was larger and heavier. A sound of surprise and delight escaped her lips as she gently undid the wrappings to discover the Book of Hours that she had first seen in his library the day Dr. Carleton had examined Giles.

"Richard, this belongs here in Marston Hall. How can you part with such a treasure?" she asked.

He longed to tell her that she belonged there, too. But he did not. "It should belong to one who loves it. I have been well aware since the day when you discovered it in my library that it would be treasured by you. It is given with gratitude for your concern and care for Giles." Richard's voice carried a sincerity to it that matched his apology and Katherine rewarded him with a smile of total happiness. The sapphires in the earrings were no match for the sparkle in her eyes. Richard sat back in his chair and secretly nurtured a hope in his heart.

The family sang Christmas carols and feasted on an elegant dinner that Cook had spent days preparing. There was smoked salmon with creamy dill sauce, roast goose, mutton, and lobster patties. Cakes and puddings were followed by ices, fruit, and cheeses, and every course was served with its proper wine from the marquess's well-stocked cellar. The men chose not to linger over port but to join the ladies directly and it was a satisfied party that retired to the salon.

Katherine curled up in a chair next to the fire and carefully examined the exquisite, infinitely delicate designs decorating her book. Richard stretched his legs out before the fire, sipping a brandy and watching Katherine's delight at every page. She often looked up and excitedly showed him some detail that was of special interest.

Paul Spencer and Lady Amelia were deep in conversation at the far end of the room. Neither Katherine nor Richard noticed, for they were too comfortable in each other's company.

The rest of the afternoon and evening was spent in the same harmony. After tea had been brought in and served, it was not long before both Amelia and Paul excused themselves. Katherine and Richard merely nodded agreement and continued to enjoy each other's company.

The embers were low when Katherine rose to bid Richard good night. "Thank you for a wonderful day. Your gifts were far too grand but I shall love and cherish them both."

Richard rose and stepped closer to her. He stood motionless for a moment, as if hesitating. Katherine raised her face to his, and that was all he needed. He reached for her and she came willingly to his arms. His lips covered hers swiftly and lovingly and pulled her closer. When she rested her head against his chest, she could hear his pounding heart.

"Oh, Katherine . . ." He kissed her again and again. Her pulse quickened to match his and her legs seemed as though they would not support her. She remained in his arms, lost in the feel of his caresses until he gently moved away.

His glittering brown-green eyes proclaimed the passion she herself felt, and he put his arm around her shoulder as he gently guided her toward the door.

"I shall not make the same mistake twice, my love," he whispered in her ear as he kissed her once more. "If I remain a moment longer, I will not have the willpower to do otherwise," he added huskily.

Katherine gave him a weak smile and made to leave through the door he had just opened.

"Good night, my love, sleep well," he said, and his low resonant voice enveloped her whole body.

"Yes, Richard . . . good night," she replied, feeling like a child about to be dismissed. She climbed the stairs, weak-kneed and a hint of tears brimming in her eyes. As Megan helped her mistress get ready for bed, she wondered at Katherine's subdued mood.

Later, Katherine lay in bed and recounted the

incident, still yearning to feel his arms around her. He had been right to send her to bed, of course, but she felt so empty. She longed to be his, totally and irrevocably. She took comfort in the fact that he had called her his love. Yet he had let her go. She remembered his vow to protect her while she was under his roof. She knew he was right, but it didn't stop her longing for him. If this is love, then why does it hurt so, she wondered.

She had never felt this way toward Giles. Giles had been flirtatious and fun, but there was a vast difference in the way she felt toward Richard. Her desire for him was all-consuming and she was lost in her longing to be his. Was this proper? Did everyone feel this way? She did not think so from the remarks she had heard about a woman's duty to her husband. She had heard it was distasteful, but a duty one must endure. Endure! She could have remained in his arms forever. Was she a wanton or just in love? He had let her go. Were his feelings as engaged as hers?

Katherine wondered about his feelings for Lucinda. No one ever mentioned her. Was Richard still in love with his dead wife? She was well aware that men needed women for their physical needs, but usually satisfied them with a mistress or lightskirt. A gentleman of Richard's fiber did not dally with members of his family, even the widow of his brother. A small nagging thought entered her mind. There was a time when she would have thought Richard most capable of such behavior. Especially when he first met her and so bluntly rejected her as a mere adventuress. That still hurt, and she wondered if her attraction to Richard was now allowing her to ignore his faults. She decided she must be more careful, lest she be hurt again.

Chapter 21

During the week between Christmas and the New Year relations between Richard and Katherine were extremely amicable. He treated her lightly and with teasing humor, though not with the overwhelming charm that had been Giles's, for Richard was far more serious by nature. Still, he showed her every kindness while not pressing her in any romantic way.

Katherine was rather perplexed by this and raised her guard a little. She was able to return the light, seemingly unconcerned attitude, and actually found it easier for her to deal with her feelings toward Richard.

Lady Amelia and Dr. Spencer exchanged approving glances more than once. They could see and feel the harmony between Richard and Katherine. It pleased them both, though they were discreet enough to show no obvious response.

On the first of the new year, Paul Spencer prepared to return to Dover. Katherine knew she would miss him dreadfully but her feelings were so strong for Richard that she could not find it in her heart to leave with her father.

Richard announced he would travel with Dr. Spencer as far as Alnwick, declaring he had business there and would return in two days' time.

He put one of his coaches at Dr. Spencer's disposal, and once their luggage was loaded, Katherine tearfully kissed her beloved father good-bye. "Father, do come again soon. I will miss you terribly," she cried, giving him one last hug before he entered the waiting coach.

Richard, who had chosen to ride outside the carriage despite the frosty air, swung himself into the saddle and gave Kate a salute. "I'll be back soon." He seemed to wish to say more, but he did not.

Kate stood on the steps with Amelia, her heart sinking as she waved farewell to the two men she loved most. She turned to reenter the house. Amelia could see the distress on Katherine's face and she put her arm around her shoulder. "He will return soon," she said. "Let us have a comfortable coz, for we have not had the time to do so lately and we must plan your move to Merrywood."

"Yes, I suppose so. Amelia, it will be ages before I see my father again. He becomes so involved in his work. I shall miss him dreadfully!" Katherine complained.

Amelia took her seat in the family salon and rang for tea. "Actually, I was thinking of Richard. He will be gone but a few days," she said.

Katherine looked up into Lady Amelia's keen brown eyes. "Does it show that much?"

"Not to most, I'm sure. But your father and I are well aware of your feelings. In fact, I approve very much. Richard's marriage to Lucinda was most unfortunate. I cannot for the life of me fathom why he chose her; they were so unsuited. He is a man to whom I have always attributed much good common sense. I suppose men sometimes cannot see beyond a pretty face."

"Tell me about Lucinda, Amelia. It all is so secret. Are you sure he does not wear the willow for her? I often detect a sadness in him," Katherine said.

"My child, it is not for me to explain Richard's feelings toward his dead wife. He must do that himself. But I can give you my observations," Amelia said. It appeared to Katherine she was weighing her words before she spoke.

"Lucinda died by drowning in the river. There has been much speculation whether it was suicide. The authorities ruled it to be an accident. It is assumed she fell from her horse and was stunned and could not save herself. The water was very shallow," Amelia continued.

Katherine, totally absorbed, did not move or take her eyes from Amelia's face.

"There are even a few—Lady Rawlins, for example—who claim it was Richard's fault." The elderly lady paused as one of the footman carried in the tea tray.

"You mean, they think he murdered her?" Katherine asked incredulously when the servant had gone.

"Not precisely, but perhaps they think he drove her to it. She was desperately unhappy," Amelia explained.

"Why? She had her baby and surely Richard would . . ." Kate's words trailed off.

Amelia gave her an indulgent smile. How love blinds and hate magnifies, she thought.

"Their marriage was over as soon as it began. I am not sure of the circumstances but Richard and Lucinda barely spoke to one another."

"Ellen? Is that why Richard does not care for the child? Although I do think he is becoming fond of her."

"Kate, some of these questions are beyond my ability to answer. It will be up to Richard to do so. But I doubt he will. He has put Lucinda from his mind. He does not like to dwell on the past, I am sure," she replied.

Katherine nodded, but her interest in the subject was now even more pronounced. She simply had to know why Richard's first marriage had been so unhappy.

During Richard's absence, Katherine began her move to Merrywood. Amelia planned to depart for Bath at the end of the week and wished to have Katherine settled before her leave-taking.

The move was fairly simple. Katherine's clothes and personal items were carefully packed and transported by cart. The same was done for Nanny Burke's and Ellen's possessions. Favorite toys were carefully collected for Ellen's new nursery.

Since Merrywood was fully furnished, no furniture needed to be transported. The staff would have to be increased beyond the few servants that had been needed only to maintain the premises, but the servants were delighted at the prospect of a family residing again in the lovely country home.

The housekeeper, Mrs. Greeves, worried about the preparations. She wanted everything to be perfect for Mrs. Swynford. Merrywood had been without a mistress for too many years and she had had only herself to please. Her worries were unnecessary, however, for her standards were very high and the house gleamed with the look of a very carefully tended home.

Katherine was supervising the packing when Latimer announced that one of the Mr. Roberts had called and wished to speak to either Lord Marston or herself. Richard had not yet returned, so Katherine rose and smoothed her skirts. She gave a quick look in the mirror and straightened her hair. Walking swiftly down the stairs to the blue salon where the barrister stood waiting, she wondered what he wished to see her about.

"Good day to you Mrs. Swynford. I am surprised to have missed Lord Marston for I am sure he knew of my arrival. At any rate, I have business with you also." The small bespectacled man withdrew a folded packet from his coat.

"Here is the final copy of the late Captain Swynford's will. All the necessary provisions have been carried out. I need your signature and then can leave your copy, which I advise you to store away safely," he said.

Katherine took the paper and slowly walked over to the settee by the fire and sat down.

"I'm sure you will find it all in order," he said nervously.

"Of course, I have no doubt of that," she replied as she continued to read Giles's will. Richard had not shown it to her and she was naturally curious. Mr. Roberts shifted a bit as he waited.

A flush crept up Katherine's face and she looked up at the slender man. "I see that I have the use of Merrywood only during my lifetime. It then goes to Ellen Swynford upon my death. Is that so? Any possible heirs I might have would have no claim on the property?" she asked, trying to control her voice.

"Yes, that is so. However, you have been settled with a comfortable allowance and should not want for anything in your lifetime," he anxiously replied. He ran a finger nervously along his collar. He wished Lord Marston were here to explain.

Just then Mr. Palmer, Lord Marston's secretary, entered the room. "May I be of assistance?" he asked. He was surprised that the attorney had arrived while his lordship was gone on business and then proceeded to closet himself with the captain's widow.

"No, I have been enlightened about the contents of this document already," Katherine said, dismissing Richard's secretary. He did not immediately leave. Katherine gave him a closed look and rose. She took the pen and wrote her signature on both the copies. Taking her own, she nodded a curt good day and quickly left the room.

"How is it you are here today? I am sure Lord Marston did not expect you," Mr. Palmer said with apprehension. He had been aware that his lordship had carefully kept the contents of the will from Mrs. Swynford. Though he did not know why, he was worried that a mistake had been made.

Katherine's hands were shaking as she climbed the stairs holding the document. Entering her room, she dismissed all the servants and sat down to reread the contents of the will. Why had Richard hidden the provision about Merrywood from her? Not that she objected to it, for she knew many widows were given the use of a home only for their lifetime. But why hide who actually would inherit it? Did he still think she was an opportunist who would try to take Ellen's inheritance from her?

If Ellen inherits the land, then Richard really has control over the considerable property, she thought. She shook her head at the idea of Richard seeking the land for his gain. He had enough of his own; he was a vastly wealthy man. Still, some men were greedy and never satisfied. No, no, that simply did not fit Richard. Or did it? She knew he stood to gain several large holdings from Lucinda's portion but had heard no more on that account. She was utterly mystified.

Anger slowly began to build inside her. Either he thought she would challenge the will for her own gain or he was after the land himself. In either case, he was abominable. The secretive, hateful man. Damn him for using his charm to sway her from examining the will at the time of Giles's death. Well, let him think she was an adventuress. She would keep a wide berth of him from now on. She would return to Dover.

Katherine thought of Ellen and buried her face in her hands and cried. She allowed herself that luxury for about five minutes. Then, quickly rising, she summoned the servants and set them to work. She called Nanny Burke, giving her instructions to get Ellen ready. They were leaving immediately for Merrywood.

Amelia came fluttering into the bedroom as Katherine was giving final instructions. "My dear, what is the rushing all about?" Amelia asked.

"I leave for Merrywood now. What is not packed can be brought later," Katherine replied tersely.

"My heavens, what is all the hurry for?" the elderly lady questioned in a confused manner.

"I will not stay in this house one minute longer. Lord Marston will be most pleased to know 'the adventuress' has quit his hallowed halls," she answered, with smoldering anger.

"I shall join you tomorrow. I cannot be ready now," Amelia answered, totally perplexed.

"This has nothing to do with you, dear lady. Just inform that arrogant martinet I will not dance to his strings. Also tell him the adventuress bids him farewell and asks him to announce all his calls prior to his arrival." She swung around, picking up her cape.

Katherine issued a stream of constant orders until she was finally assisted into the carriage. Ellen and Nanny Burke sat across from her, watching in silence as the fur robes were placed on their laps and legs to protect them from the chill. The footman bowed and closed up the steps. The coachman swung up on the box and two outriders mounted their horses. Then, they were off in a swirl of dry dust and dead leaves.

Amelia stood at the window, clutching a fine lawn handkerchief to her chest. Great heavens, what was this all about? What would she tell Richard? Exactly what Katherine had said? The waters run deep here, she thought.

Richard returned to Marston Hall just after dusk. He was amazed to hear that Katherine had already taken up residence at Merrywood. He learned Ellen and Nanny Burke accompanied her, if all the trunks did not.

Amelia motioned Richard into the salon and closed

the door. "Richard, the child left in a fury, I tell you," she exclaimed.

"Really? Whatever for? Did she tell you the reason?" he asked.

"No! She told me to tell you that . . . Oh, my." She faltered.

"Damn it, Aunt Amelia, tell me," Richard said as his patience began to be tested.

"She said . . . she said . . ."

"Yes, she said what?" he fairly shouted.

"She said you would be happy to know the adventuress had quit your hallowed halls . . ." Amelia burst into a wail of tears.

Richard's eyes flashed with a cold green glint and he let loose a string of oaths that Amelia had never heard before. He turned on her. "What happened that made her fly off this way?"

"I don't know. Ask Mr. Palmer, he was with your solicitor and Katherine this afternoon."

"The devil take it." He strode to the doorway. "Mr. Palmer!" he bellowed down the hall. He met the young man scurrying down the long corridor.

"Come to the study at once," he commanded.

He was quickly obeyed. "Now tell me. Was Roberts here today? What transpired?"

Mr. Palmer related the part of the events that he had witnessed.

Richard ran his hand through his hair and paced the room a moment. "You should have taken care of the matter. That fool Roberts. Well, whatever she's taken offense at, I'll have to set it right."

"I'm sorry, my lord. They were in conversation before I arrived," the young man tried to explain. He fairly quaked at the fury of the marquess's face.

"I want to see that fool Roberts as soon as possible. Now please leave me, Palmer," Richard commanded.

After Palmer had gone, Richard stood silent a

moment with his hands behind his back and his feet slightly parted. He looked for the world like a man about to conquer the world. His eyes flashed with anger. He tried to convince himself that all could be explained easily. It was just that he did not want Kate to know about Giles and Lucinda. Damn, his careful plans certainly had gone awry.

Chapter 22

Early the next morning, Richard set out for Merry-wood. The spring mist hung close to the ground, casting an eerie gray on the budding trees as he rode his horse hard and fast through the countryside. The air was chilly and he turned his collar up along his neck. His handsome face was set in determination and his eyes were as cold as ice as he neared his destination.

Swinging down from the saddle, he quickly tethered his great stallion, not even waiting for a groom to take the horse. Swiftly mounting the steps and crossing the small terrace, he reached for the brass door knocker. The impatient clapping of the knocker reverberated through the hall entrance, sending the butler, Vernon, scurrying to admit the impatient visitor. He opened the door slowly and was momentarily taken aback by the ferocious scowl set upon the face of the marquess.

Vernon had no allegiance to Lord Marston, and therefore he very carefully followed his mistress's instructions. "Lord Marston, Mrs. Swynford is not receiving guests. She requests that in the future you please send a message announcing your intention to call, so satisfactory arrangements concerning Miss Ellen can be made," Vernon said, firmly blocking the entrance.

Richard's anger flared, and with the suddenness of a bolt of lightning, he swept the totally surprised butler from his path. "You are mistaken. Mrs. Swynford is receiving *this* guest," he announced as he rushed past the butler to take the stairs two at a time.

"Katherine, it is I, Richard. Come to call! Do you hear me? I'm announcing my intention, loud and clear," he bellowed as he bounded up the stairs.

Vernon, having been almost knocked off his feet, stood aghast. As quickly as his short legs could carry him, he went in search of Norton. He knew well enough Katherine's faithful protector could handle the irate Lord Marston.

He was slightly out of breath when he found Norton sitting over a huge breakfast, sipping tea and teasing with the blushing cook. "Lord Marston is here! He's taken to the boughs! Almost knocked me off my feet, he did, when I refused him entrance," the red-faced butler puffed.

Norton looked up in surprise. "Indeed? And why is that?" he asked.

"I don't have the foggiest, but he bounded up the stairs to see Mrs. Swynford yelling at the top of his lungs that she'd see him or else!"

Norton smiled, his crinkly eyes dancing. "Hmmm."

"You must *do* something!" the butler insisted.

"I imagine Mrs. Swynford can handle this matter to her own satisfaction. I'll not intrude." Norton chuckled. For the second time in a few minutes, Vernon's jaw dropped in shock.

Up in Kate's room, Megan was brushing her mistress's long dark hair when they heard what sounded like someone yelling. Katherine rose from the chair at the commotion in the hallway and opened her door to investigate what all the noise was about. She moved to the upper hall just in time to see Richard Swynford mounting the steps, calling her name. His face flushed with anger and fire was in his eyes.

"Richard! Whatever are you causing this ruckus about?" Katherine asked as he ran down the hall to her side. He looked so ridiculous, she almost smiled.

"You, my dear, you!" he snapped, grabbing her by the arm and almost dragging her into her bedroom. He was so tall, her feet fairly dangled on the floor as she struggled to keep up with him.

"Leave us, Megan," he ordered. Megan glanced at her mistress in uncertainty. Richard, still holding Katherine firmly by her arm, glared at the cowering maid.

"Did you hear me? Megan, get out!" Richard fairly shouted.

The maid scampered from the room as fast as her legs could carry her, her eyes as big as saucers. Picking up her skirts, she ran to find Norton.

"Richard! How dare you! The servants will have enough gossip to last a week. Whatever is this about?" she admonished.

"This," he said as he kicked the door closed. He pulled her into his arms and very thoroughly kissed her. Katherine's resistance was nil. She returned his kisses with enthusiasm.

"Now, madame, do I have *permission* to call on you?" he mocked as he stepped back. His hazel eyes flashed green and brown and Katherine stood gazing at them. The barest hint of a smile appeared around her mouth.

"Oh," Katherine weakly uttered. All her anger had melted with a kiss. He certainly could erase all practical thoughts from a lady's head, she thought. Her face flushed scarlet as she struggled for something to say.

"Well, what is this nonsense about?" he asked, and he again placed his hands on her shoulders. His hazel-green eyes held her own eyes as if by command.

"The will. You didn't tell me," she softly answered.

"Didn't tell you what? That you had use of the house during your lifetime and that afterward it went to Ellen? Does that bother you?" he asked.

"Of course not! I'm not the opportunist you have accused me of being. I just don't like the implication that hiding the provision from me has. Unless it's yourself that is benefiting by the land coming into your hands." She threw the words back at him and felt his hands tighten their grip on her shoulders.

"You little fool! You have so little faith for such an innocent!" he chided, and once again covered her mouth with his. His hands caressed her back and he trailed kisses down her neck. When Katherine looked into his eyes again, they were clouded with passion and the keen glitter was gone.

"Kate, there is much I will tell you someday, but not now. Now is not the time." He seemed to hesitate.

He let her go. "Don't ever put up a wall between us again. There is none big enough to keep me from you. You will be mine. You belong to me. Even Giles knew that," he said, his voice soft with passion.

Richard did not await her reply, but turned and left the room. Katherine stood in the spot he had left her, listening to his spurred boots click down the stairs, across the hall, and out of the manor. She pressed her hand against her mouth, her blood pounding through her veins and in her temples. A flood of happiness spread through her body. He had claimed her as his own and in her heart she knew that she had always been his since the first time she had laid eyes on him.

The servants spent hours speculating on Lord Marston's interest in his brother's wife. The story of how he stormed into the house to her bedroom was told over and over and all the while Norton smiled and kept his counsel.

The speculation died very soon, however, as Richard

did not immediately call again. This amazing fact brought Katherine first disbelief, then a string of oaths that would do a camel driver justice. She could not fathom why he would cover her with kisses, swear she belonged to him, and then never come to call. She decided the Swynfords had a streak of insanity in their family.

I shall not waste one more moment's thought on him, she vowed. Between making plans for renovating the manor and caring for Ellen, who had come down with a cold, she actually did rather well in forgetting about him until the day she met him while riding.

Katherine was still in mourning and wore a black riding habit. The hat was smart with a black feather that curled along her cheek. Her cheeks were rosy with the chill of early spring and her eyes sparkled as they always did when she abandoned herself to riding over the moors. Giles had been right; she loved the north country.

He was in the company of Lady Hampton when she came upon him. Katherine was dismayed at how beautiful that elegant lady looked in her dress of blue velvet trimmed in black fox.

Lord Marston greeted Katherine with genuine interest, giving her his devastating smile. "Good morning, Kate. How are you faring? How is Ellen?" he asked, leveling his intense eyes on her.

Katherine scoffed and sent him a scathing look. "Your interest is overwhelming! How very kind of you to inquire. Your daughter has a slight cold but is on the mend. And as you know, I always manage to land on my feet."

Richard crooked an eyebrow and softly chuckled. Lady Hampton turned toward him in surprise, for she had thought Katherine extremely rude.

Immediately understanding that Richard knew she was annoyed by his lack of attention, Katherine was furious with herself for being so transparent. "It has been an undeniable pleasure to see you both and certainly educational. I now must return to Merrywood," she said with as much hauteur as she could muster. Her cheeks blazed scarlet and her eyes glared daggers as she turned her horse to leave the couple.

"Kate, I will call to say good-bye. I leave for the Continent and shall be gone several months," Richard said before she had ridden away.

Katherine reined in the horse and raised her eyes directly to his.

"Yes, Paris and Vienna are all aglitter, with the Continent now free of the French monster. It shall be vastly amusing," Lady Hampton gushed.

Katherine's eyes still held his. She could see annoyance in their hazel depths, at Lady Hampton's remark and the muscle in his cheek tightened. "I should imagine it will be most exciting. I do hope you both have an unforgettable time, as I am sure you will." With a glistening sparkle of tears beginning to edge her eyes, she urged her horse forward.

Richard watched Katherine ride off with a sinking heart. It seemed to him, suddenly, that in every way he tried to protect her, he failed. To escape speculation he was seen occasionally with Lady Hampton. He had told Kate plainly that he kept his distance to avoid the strong attraction he felt for her. Why was she annoyed? Couldn't she see his intentions were honest? Damn, he thought, women are impossible to understand.

Lady Hampton tried desperately to gain his attention. "Richard, we are bound to meet in Paris, and I shall expect you to pay some attendance," she said, fluttering her eyes.

Richard turned his glittering gaze upon her and wished to heavens he was anywhere else. "Yes, I expect so," he replied in a dead voice, and turned his stallion homeward.

As he had promised, Richard did call within the fortnight. Katherine was with Ellen in the nursery when she was informed he was waiting to see her. She turned to take the child with her. Let the mighty Lord Marston try to melt her resistance with kisses when Ellen was present. Kate was delighted with her ploy.

He was standing by the mantel as she entered the saloon. Katherine held Ellen's hand as she smiled in cool response to his greeting.

"Papa!" Ellen exclaimed as she broke loose and ran to Richard's arms. He picked her up and hugged her, placing a kiss on the child's cheek. His eyes met Katherine's.

"Do you feel safer with her in attendance?" he asked Kate.

"Yes, my lord, or with Lady Hampton. Since she is not with you today, I shall hide behind Ellen's skirts."

"I never thought you to be the coward." He smiled.

"With you, sir, it is a matter of survival!" she replied hotly.

Richard smiled with that wonderful smile which almost made Kate weep openly. "Then there is hope for me," he added.

"Never! You're just a libertine! Lady Hampton suits you well."

Richard chuckled. Carrying Ellen in his arms, he walked over to Katherine. He kissed Ellen. "Papa is going to be gone for some months, but he shall get you a pony when he returns." He then turned to Katherine.

"It is impossible to be so close and yet so far. I can hardly court my brother's widow before she is out of mourning," he said as he handed Ellen to her. Richard reached out and lovingly stroked her cheek and looked deeply into her eyes. Then he bowed and turned to leave. She watched him in silence as he crossed the hall, place his hat on his rich hair, and left Merrywood without looking back.

Chapter 23

Katherine accepted Richard's words on faith. She filled her days with the activities of the large country manor and the care of Ellen.

She watched spring bloom forth, and as she walked among the daffodils, primroses, and violets she thought of Giles. She was hardly able to bring his image to mind, which chagrined her for it had been only a year since they rode together on the shores of Dover. She realized he had been only a moment in her life, but she felt remorse that he had faded into a vague memory. So much had transpired in the year. Had she changed so much? How young she had been!

Guilt over her failure to love Giles still lingered in her mind. Never had she felt the mature, passionate, and longing love she felt for Richard. Giles had been a light-hearted infatuation, the kind that should come to every young girl before she marries. If only she had known the difference between youthful infatuation and passionate commitment back then.

Katherine dreamed constantly of Richard. She could picture him in so many ways. The penetrating look on his face on their first encounter when he had insulted her. Katherine smiled at that memory. He had been so taken aback when he first saw her. His manly stride, and the way he suddenly turned his head when his interest was caught. There were so many images but especially she remembered the warm passion in his eyes when he held her.

He would be back for her. It would not be Lady Hampton he chose. She would patiently wait out the year.

Spring slipped into summer as Katherine oversaw the cleaning and necessary refurbishing of every room in Merrywood. The house was not in disrepair but it needed the keen eye of a mistress to bring it up to standards. The brass and silver now shone. The windows sparkled with clean glass. Floors glowed with new wax, and rugs had been beaten and cleaned. Katherine threw herself into the task of renovating the home, and amazed the servants with her willingness to work alongside them. She won their admiration with the example she set, and they were as proud as she was when the house was brought into order.

Finally, there remained Giles's room to set into order. It held no memories for her, since she had never lived at Merrywood with him, but the idea of sorting through his belongings put her off. But it had to be done.

She entered the chamber alone one morning. At first, she just aimlessly wandered around the room. While she could not feel it as a real part of Giles, an ominous apprehension filled her.

It was a beautiful room. Its size and decor gave it a pleasant, masculine appeal. The furniture was dark but the walls light and large windows let in the sunlight, making the room almost airy. Wondering why the room made her feel so uncomfortable, she decided it was just the knowledge it had been Giles's that disconcerted her.

She opened an armoire and ran her hands along the hanging clothes. A shiver ran down her spine. He had existed, but it all seemed so long ago, she thought. Glancing down, a chest of exquisite carved wood caught her eye and she stooped to pull it out.

Seating herself on the floor, Kate fumbled with the

household keys she had tied on her waist, but none fit the lock. She rose and walked over to the beautiful Chippendale secretary. Most of these desks had secret compartments and she ran her hand along the inside compartments. The cross member of the letter section moved slightly. How clever, she thought. This one was different than other desks she had seen. She slipped the slender wood carving out to reveal a small space in which a brass key lay. Removing the key, she replaced the wood piece and returned to the chest.

Seating herself on the floor, she tried the key in the lock. A click sounded and she raised the lid. The chest held papers and several small boxes. She pulled out a gold locket and opened it. A well-executed miniature of Lucinda smiled back at her. Katherine sat a moment staring at the shy smile of the delicately beautiful woman. Her heart skipped a beat and she felt her cheeks flush. Snapping it shut, she quickly replaced it.

An awareness began to creep over her as she reached for a packet of letters tied in a ribbon. The handwriting was precise and pretty. She slowly opened the first letter and saw it began, "My dearest Giles . . ." Katherine read on. "My longing grows for you each day. My only happiness is the knowledge that the child I carry is ours. I think life without you would be unbearable, so you must return as soon as possible. Don't let Richard force you into the army. We can be happy together. Richard is hateful, as always. He no longer even bothers to speak to me."

Katherine read each letter. Every one declared Lucinda's undying love for Giles and her longing to be with him. Weeping with shame and regret for Giles and Lucinda, Katherine sat back and closed her eyes. Ellen was Giles's daughter. Of course! Katherine could see that so plainly now. Richard—God, Richard had always known it.

She remembered her angry words to Richard when

she accused him of not caring for his own child and recalled the flicker of hurt she had seen in his eyes. How did he now feel toward Ellen? Had Richard loved Lucinda and was he heartbroken by her betrayal? Lord, how everything fell into place.

A sudden thought stabbed her heart. Had Richard made love to her to even the score with Giles? No, she knew better than that. Richard did love her and would come to her after the period of mourning was over.

Everything seemed clear, except the reason Giles had married her. He may not have loved Lucinda, but he had carefully kept her letters and tenderly put them away. Kate knew Giles had not loved her since he had told her so before he died.

What fools people are, she mused. What hell they can make of their lives. She thought of Richard and wept for his hurt.

Shaken, she slowly rose from the floor. Replacing the letters and the locket, she returned the trunk to its original place in the wardrobe and closed the doors. She slowly walked across the room, then closed and locked the door.

Katherine did not have the energy to decide what to do about the letters she had found. Once more, she found solitude in her room. She climbed on her bed and stretched out, willing herself to calm down.

But her thoughts remained in turmoil. She relived the night she had lain almost naked and very willing in Richard's arms. A quirk of fate had stopped him from taking her, or so she had assumed, until now. Richard had called her an adventuress, and so she must have seemed. She had accused him of attempting to cuckold his brother.

She covered her face with her hands. Oh, heavens, she wept, what pain we cause unknowingly.

Doubt began to creep into her. Richard had said she belonged to him, but he had never said he loved her or would marry her. Had he used her to revenge himself on Giles? She knew Richard was capable of it.

She also remembered what the groom had told her about Lucinda's death. *She had tied the horse. It was no accident.*

Would she ever know the truth? Did Lucinda commit suicide? "Oh, Richard," she cried out loud. "I need you."

Katherine continued to ponder about the meaning of what she had learned today. The implication was that Giles had been terribly selfish and dishonest. He certainly had not treated Lucinda or herself with honor. Knowing she had put the sadness of her marriage to Giles behind her, she realized how bizarre their union had been.

She thought of Dover and seriously considered returning to her father immediately. That would be a way to escape but it would never settle what, if anything, truly existed between herself and Richard.

I have suffered a difficult journey across the country, widowhood, and the knowledge that my marriage was for naught, she thought. Well, I shall see this through. I could not leave and never know if Richard and I are bound to be together. Ellen still needs me and so I shall hold to my decision. Waiting can be the most lonely of all experiences, but wait I shall.

With the hope that springs from youth, Katherine finally slept and the dreams she dreamed were of Richard.

The months passed slowly with Katherine making every effort to keep busy with the matters of the household and estate. It was surprising how much she learned in those early days and how fulfilling it was. Mr. Dorty, the bailiff, was infinitely patient. He took her about the lands and explained the working of the farms. He introduced her to the tenants and their families. She was well received everywhere, for she was personable and genuinely interested in their families. She and Dorty saw to needed repairs and improvements of the cottages. The estate had been well cared for because Dorty was honest and capable. Giles had been fortunate to have Dorty and now Katherine appreciated his faithful work. They had an excellent working relationship, even if Kate suspected Dorty sought her out on many occasions for advise on matters he could have well handled alone. It wasn't as if he patronized her. He did not. He just knew it was best to have her occupied so she didn't grieve over her loss.

Riding was a favorite pastime and Katherine often took Ellen up in front of her in the saddle to ride through the fields and meadows. The love between them grew stronger each day, binding Katherine to Merrywood more than ever.

Merrywood soon took on the look of a well-kept home. Katherine's estates were running smoothly, and the love and companionship of Ellen had filled her days. She was almost happy.

However, Richard was never far from her mind and she longed to see him. He did not write and that was a disappointment, one that she could not understand. He had gone because he had said he could not stand to have her so near yet be unable to be with her. She knew she could not court her while she was in mourning, for that would cast a suspicion neither of them wanted. Society placed such stock on what it termed propriety. She would wait.

The mystery of Lucinda haunted Katherine and she still wondered if her death had been an accident or a suicide. One morning she was about to mount her horse for a ride, when she turned to McGuire, the head groom.

"Would you ride out with me this morning?" she asked.

"Aye, my lady," he replied as he slipped off his

leather apron. He was a bit surprised by the request but happy to oblige her. He was a small Irishman, who had no peer in his ability to handle horses, especially the racers which had been Giles's passion.

He saddled up a fine stallion that needed exercise and met Katherine in the stableyard. "Where would ye like ta ride?" he asked with a grin that brought out the smile lines in his leathery features.

"Mr. McGuire, will you show me where Lady Marston had her accident? I would rather you did not speak to anyone about my request, but I am curious," she said in a soft voice, filled with embarrassment.

He nodded. He understood her curiosity. "Be happy to. 'Tis only natural. I'll not speak of it. We'll head down to the river, to Fall's Bridge."

It was not a long ride, but it was a beautiful one. Ancient oaks lined much of the lane, their branches meeting overhead in a cathedral-like arch. But Katherine paid little heed to the scenery, for she was interested only in what the groom had to show her.

They came out into a clearing along the small river-bank and Katherine could hear the faint rush of water. Trailing after McGuire on the small track, she reined in her horse as he halted at a small bridge just above a short waterfall.

McGuire turned his keen eyes to her and nodded his head in the direction of the water.

"Here?" she asked.

"Aye," he said.

"But it's so shallow! You could stand at least waist high!"

"Aye, and the horse was tied," he added quietly.

"Then it couldn't have been an accident unless she was knocked out or some such thing," Kate said.

"She had no marks on her to indicate a fall," he replied. "It was suicide plain and simple," he added.

"But it was declared an accident," she said.

"I'm sure that was to protect his lordship from scandal." McGuire knew that to be true, for he himself had untied the horse.

"Why?" she asked.

"Because he is a good man," McGuire said simply. He had seen Giles with Lucinda, and had kept it to himself, but he had been compelled to protect Lord Marston as best he could.

Katherine looked over to McGuire. "You untied the horse."

He did not answer at first. "Lord Marston was innocent in this matter and did not deserve gossip."

Tears brimmed in Kate's eyes. "Let us quit this place. Thank you for bringing me."

"Aye, Mrs. Swynford, it is best now to let the past be buried," he sagely answered.

They turned their horses homeward without any more conversation.

Chapter 24

Katherine stood looking out of the nursery window. The rain had stopped during the night and a pale sun glowed softly through the smoky mist, giving the illusion of weak warmth to the late October morning. Droplets of water glistened on the panes and the last of the golden leaves clung precariously to the oaks. She could see the garden and the mums still lingered soddenly against the brick walls. Even one or two roses hung on tenaciously to the last of the fair weather. Winter weather came early off the North Sea and these last autumn days were lingering just a big longer.

It was just over a year since Giles had died. Restlessly pressing her hand down the folds of her black dress, she turned to Ellen.

"Ellen, the weather is clearing. Would you like to ride with me? I will take you up on Marigold. We might take a short ride if you wish," she said.

Nanny Burke looked up at her mistress and understood her restlessness. It must be lonely for one so young here without her family and all, she mused. True, the young woman had made Merrywood her home, and a fine job of that she did. She supposed Mrs. Swynford could not help but be lonely for someone her own age. Nanny felt a pang of sorrow for the young woman.

"Oh, Aunt Kate, do let us go," Ellen said, jumping up with excitement. "It's such fun to ride up with you.

It's so high!" Ellen's enthusiasm spread through the nursery and Kate and Nanny Burke smiled.

"Dress Ellen warmly, Nanny, for I fear it is far cooler than the pale sun informs us," Katherine said as she left to change into her riding habit.

Megan was busy bustling about Kate's bedchamber.

"I'm taking Ellen for a ride," she said as she paused a moment before the mirror. Kate's hand went to her face as she critically viewed her reflection. She'd changed. There was a maturity in the eyes that stared back at her.

"Well, it's of no matter," she said aloud. Megan looked to her mistress not understanding the remark. Opening the wardrobe, the maid withdrew the black habit.

Kate stood a moment looking at it. "No, Megan, bring out the blue habit," she said. Megan nodded, a bit surprised.

A year had passed and it was time to come out of mourning. Katherine took the smart habit from Megan and held it up for a moment. She removed her black gown, took up the blue skirt, stepped into it, and fastened it. She was about to began a new period in her life, and as she slipped into the jacket, it seemed to represent the future.

A sparkle entered Katherine's eyes as she donned the blue habit. Happily placing its jaunty hat upon her head at a decidedly rakish angle, she allowed a small laugh to escape her lips.

"My gracious, can this be me?" she teased, preening a bit before the mirror.

"Aye, and as you should be," Megan agreed.

Taking Ellen from Nanny, Katherine almost skipped down the stairs and out to the stableyard. McGuire smiled at the merry air of the ladies and helped Katherine mount her horse. She took Ellen up before her in the saddle and cantered out of the stableyard.

The air was brisk, so Katherine did not go far. She rode along the park edge and Ellen laughed in delight the whole way. Kate held the child close and snuggled her close against her chest, feeling joyful for the first time in a year. Her spirits soared.

As they returned to the stableyard, Kate reached down and kissed Ellen on the side of her cheek. As she raised her head, her eyes met those of someone leaning against the paddock fence. Her heart gave a lurch.

"Papa! Papa!" squealed Ellen in delight, and Katherine almost lost the squirming child.

Richard straightened up and smiled. He strode over to the horse and reached up for Ellen. His eyes rose to Katherine's and she thought she might faint. The horse responded to Katherine's reaction and fidgeted. She pulled in the reins as Richard took the child in his arms.

"Hello, my little love. Give Papa a kiss," he said, planting one on the laughing child's cheek. Ellen's little arms flew around Richard's neck and she hugged him with glee.

Richard looked up at Katherine. They did not speak. Tears brimmed up in her eyes.

He set Ellen down and took Katherine by her waist and lifted her slowly from the saddle. A groom came running to take the horse.

"Hello," he whispered.

"Richard . . ." She faltered as the tears threatened to spill over.

She looked up at his profile. His face was thinner and seemed more chiseled and even a little harsher. He turned to her and the warmth of his hazel eyes softened the austere look.

"Kate, you look wonderful," he said.

He picked Ellen up in one arm and put the other around Kate's waist as they slowly walked toward the house. No words were spoken between them. It was as if they had to savor the moment. Ellen chattered away, and though no one was listening, she didn't seem to notice.

"Come see what I brought my two favorite ladies from Paris," he teased.

He led them into the family salon and picked up a large white box tied with blue ribbon. He knelt down before Ellen and presented it to her. Inside was yet another doll. A miniature Queen Bess, it was dressed in an embroidered blue gown that was studded with pearls and had a ruff and lace collar.

"From Paris?" Kate laughed.

"The way the English are flocking to Paris, it is clever business of the French," he replied with a smile. "The economy is in shambles, as well you can imagine. The bread lines are pitiful." He shook his head, then clapped his hands.

"Never mind that. For today is special," he said.

"Why, Papa?" Ellen asked.

"Why, simply because I'm home for good, my pet," he triumphantly announced as he rang for Nanny Burke.

"I wish to speak to you alone, Kate," he said. Katherine could not take her eyes off him. He was as wonderful as she had remembered. She flushed with excitement and her hands trembled as she removed her hat.

"I should change, Richard," she said.

"I'll not let you out of my sight yet," he ordered, not caring for a moment if Nanny Burke heard his words as she ushered her charge from the room. Nanny heard all right, and before Richard had time to launch into his intended topic with Kate, so had every servant in the lower hall.

Richard closed the door tightly and smiled over to Katherine as he did so. She understood and returned the smile when she heard the click of the lock.

"This time, my love, there will be no interruptions."

Katherine flushed, feeling a warmth rush through her body as he crossed the room. He reached out his arms to her and without a word she ran to him. His arms encircled her completely; she could hardly breathe. They stood thus, for some moments, just holding on to each other.

Richard raised his hand and stroked her hair. "Kate, it's been an eternity waiting for you. There were times I almost came to claim you, the waiting was so unbearable."

"Oh, Richard, I've thought of you constantly. Why didn't you write?"

"I tried but I couldn't. My longing would have shown and made it even more unbearable. I knew you understood."

Katherine hadn't understood, but refrained from telling him how she had longed for a word from him. But she acknowledged that if the letters had been full of longing and love, it would have been, as he had said, unbearable. If they had been newsy, she would have despaired.

He continued to hold her. "Richard, I found letters from Lucinda to Giles, and now I understand . . ."

"Did you burn them?" he interrupted.

"No, I didn't know what—"

"Do so as soon as possible. That is all behind us now."

He kissed the side of her temple and whispered, "Katherine, can this be really true? Are you really, finally in my arms, or is this another of my many dreams?"

Kate laughed softly. "I'm here, Richard, believe me, I *know* I'm in your arms."

His hand slid down the side of her face and his thumb traced her jaw and lips as he raised her face to his.

She looked into those marvelous thickly lashed eyes,

pale hazel with flecks of green and yellow. The tenderness in them filled her heart.

"Oh, Richard . . ."

He bent his head and his mouth covered hers tenderly. "I'm afraid to ever let you go." He kissed her again, this time with growing passion. He probed her mouth with his tongue, kissed her eyes, her neck and her mouth again. Katherine clung to him and returned every kiss with equal passion. He slid his hands down her back and pressed her closer.

"Kate, we must marry and marry soon!" His husky voice was muffled as he kissed and spoke at the same time. His breath tickled her neck and she giggled. Richard looked down.

"My proposal amuses you?" he teased.

"No, your kisses."

"Then I should improve upon them." He laughed.

She reached up around his neck and on tiptoes planted a well executed kiss of her own.

"Does this mean, Mrs. Swynford that you have consented to become Lady Marston?" he asked.

"Of course—it's an obvious step up the aristocratic ladder. But are you sure you want an adventuress for a wife?" she teased.

"Am I never to be forgiven that?" he said with mock helplessness.

"Never! I assure you, never. Unless, of course, you finish what you began on that previous occasion. I just might then concede to forget and forgive."

"Your charge is a very easy task. You inspire the highest motivation. Say when you will marry me, so that I can proceed to earn my forgiveness."

"Tomorrow?" she boldly replied.

"Ah, I am correct. You *are* an adventuress, and I suspect my life with you will be just one adventure after another." He pulled a leather box from his pocket and opened it to reveal a large, square-cut diamond set on a ring. "This makes it official," he said.

"Richard! It's magnificent! I've never seen one so large. I mean, it's enormous!" she said, absolutely overwhelmed.

"My dear, nothing else would be appropriate for such a temptress." He smiled tenderly. "I'd say it borders on just this side of vulgar."

"My lord, it was you who set the scene. I was just an innocent victim," she teased.

"Innocent now, but my love, not for long. If Giles did one good thing in his life, it was to bring you to me."

"No, Richard, two. He gave us Ellen," she softly reminded him.

Richard was silent a moment. "Yes, and we will put the past behind us, for we will be a real family now. One that I suspect will become exceedingly large."

"Why so?" she said as she smiled delightedly.

"Katherine, you must know the only way to keep an adventuress at home is to provide her with such a brood, she has no time to go adventuring," Richard said with mock seriousness.

He pulled her close and kissed her again and again.

"Richard, if you intend to behave like this, there isn't an adventuress in the world who could keep up with you. I'll not have time to catch my breath."

"Exactly," he replied. "That is my intention."

"Tomorrow?"

"Aye, tomorrow. I've waited long enough, Kate, and I'll not take the chance of losing this most enchanting witch who has cast a spell on me."

"Witch? Not adventuress now?"

"That, too," he said, and his mouth once more covered hers as he proceeded to finish the task set before him.